March's menu
BARONESSA GELATERIA
in Boston's North End

In addition to all our regular flavors of Italian gelato, this month we are featuring:

• Chocolate cake drizzled with hot caramel

With a rebellious lock of soft brown hair over his amber-flecked eyes, Flint Kingman had only to look at a woman to have her do his bidding. Until Gina Barone stepped onto his client list. Now he summoned her onto his turf and prepared for a battle of the sexes.

• A slice of baked Alaska

Gina Barone worked in a man's world—and knew the male of the species. She would shed her icy persona and become the sultry she-devil in their pretend affair, just as Flint wanted. Then she would burn *him*.

• Flesh-burning three-alarm chili

A wet kiss, an erotic pose…Flint and Gina put on a good show for the paparazzi. But who was more surprised by the genuine heat rising from the pictures—the proper Bostonians, the Barone family…or the couple themselves?

Buon appetito!

Dear Reader,

In honor of International Women's Day, March 8, celebrate romance, love and the accomplishments of women all over the world by reading six passionate, powerful and provocative new titles from Silhouette Desire.

New York Times bestselling author Sharon Sala leads the Desire lineup with *Amber by Night* (#1495). A shy librarian uses her alter ego to win her lover's heart in a sizzling love story by this beloved MIRA and Intimate Moments author. Next, a pretend affair turns to true passion when a Barone heroine takes on the competition, in *Sleeping with Her Rival* (#1496) by Sheri WhiteFeather, the third title of the compelling DYNASTIES: THE BARONES saga.

A single mom shares a heated kiss with a stranger on New Year's Eve and soon after reencounters him at work, in *Renegade Millionaire* (1497) by Kristi Gold. *Mail-Order Prince in Her Bed* (#1498) by Kathryn Jensen features an Italian nobleman who teaches an American ingenue the language of love, while a city girl and a rancher get together with the help of her elderly aunt, in *The Cowboy Claims His Lady* (#1499) by Meagan McKinney, the latest MATCHED IN MONTANA title. And a contractor searching for his secret son finds love in the arms of the boy's adoptive mother, in *Tangled Sheets, Tangled Lies* (#1500) by brand-new author Julie Hogan, debuting in the Desire line.

Delight in all six of these sexy Silhouette Desire titles this month…and every month.

Enjoy!

Joan Marlow Golan

Joan Marlow Golan
Senior Editor, Silhouette Desire

Please address questions and book requests to:
Silhouette Reader Service
U.S.: 3010 Walden Ave., P.O. Box 1325, Buffalo, NY 14269
Canadian: P.O. Box 609, Fort Erie, Ont. L2A 5X3

Sleeping with Her Rival

SHERI WHITEFEATHER

Silhouette Desire

Published by Silhouette Books

America's Publisher of Contemporary Romance

Special thanks and acknowledgment are given
to Sheri WhiteFeather for her contribution to the
DYNASTIES: THE BARONES series.

To Silhouette, for inviting me to do this project. To the other *Dynasties* authors
and our editor, Mavis Allen, for being such a joy to work with. To
Frank Cardinal, my *primo* dad, for introducing me to Italian delis, Italian words
and Italian humor. To Rick Bundy, my very special second dad, for inspiring the
classic Corvette and the *Caine Mutiny* in this book. To Joanne Rice, my cousin,
and Flora and Mary Yacabucci, my great aunts, for their unwavering support.
And, finally, I would like to acknowledge two remarkable teenagers—
Brenna, my beautiful "new" daughter, and Nikki, my "old-soul" son.
I love you both.

 SILHOUETTE BOOKS

ISBN 0-373-76496-0

SLEEPING WITH HER RIVAL

Books by Sheri WhiteFeather

Silhouette Desire

Warrior's Baby #1248
Skyler Hawk: Lone Brave #1272
Jesse Hawk: Brave Father #1278
Cheyenne Dad #1300
Night Wind's Woman #1332
Tycoon Warrior #1364
Cherokee #1376
Comanche Vow #1388
Cherokee Marriage Dare #1478
Sleeping with Her Rival #1496

SHERI WHITEFEATHER

lives in Southern California and enjoys ethnic dining, American Indian powwows and visiting art galleries and vintage clothing stores near the beach. Since her one true passion is writing, she is thrilled to be a part of the Silhouette Desire line. When she isn't writing, she often reads until the wee hours of the morning.

Sheri is married to a Muscogee Creek silversmith. They have a son, a daughter and a trio of cats—domestic and wild. She loves to hear from her readers. You may write to her at: P.O. Box 17146, Anaheim, California 92817.

DYNASTIES: THE BARONES

Meet the Barones of Boston—
an elite clan caught in a web of danger, deceit…and desire!

Who's Who in
SLEEPING WITH HER RIVAL

Flint Kingman—His fiery, passionate nature clashes with his stoic part-Cherokee heritage. Still, with his dark good looks and rakish smile, he is the media's darling….

Gina Barone—Her hot temper steams next to the cold shoulder she turns to everyone she views as corporate competition, including Flint Kingman. With her briefcase and her chignon, she is the ice princess….

Maria Barone—The baby of the family, she carries on all the traditions at the decades-old Baronessa Gelateria. And she carries on the family secrets, as well….

One

Gina Barone wasn't in the mood to party, but she sipped a glass of chardonnay—praying it wouldn't irritate her stomach—and worked her way through the charity mixer, feigning an I'm-in-control smile.

She knew it was important to be seen, to hold her head high, especially now. Gina was the vice president of marketing and public relations for Baronessa Gelati, a family-owned Italian ice cream empire—a company being shredded by the media.

Something Gina felt responsible for.

Moving through the crowd, she nodded to familiar faces. Although she'd come here to make her presence known, she thought it best to avoid lengthy conversations. A polite greeting was about all she could handle. And with that in mind, she would sample the food, sip a tiny bit of wine and then wait until an appropriate amount of time passed before she said her goodbyes and made a gracious exit.

"Gina?"

She stopped to acknowledge Morgan Chancellor, a business associate who flitted around the social scene like a butterfly, fluttering from one partygoer to the next.

"Oh, hello. You look lovely, Morgan. That's a beautiful dress."

"Why, thank you." The other woman batted her lashes, then leaned in close. "Do you know who asked about you?"

Gina suspected plenty of people were talking about her, about the fiasco she'd arranged last month, the Valentine's Day publicity event that had ended in disaster.

Baronessa had been launching a new flavor called passionfruit, offering a free tasting at their corporate headquarters. But pandemonium erupted when people tasted the gelato.

An unknown culprit had spiked the ice cream with a mouth-burning substance, which they'd soon discovered was habanero peppers—the hottest chilies in the world.

And worse yet, a friend of Gina's who'd stopped by the event at her invitation had suffered from an attack of anaphylaxis, a serious and rapid allergic reaction to the peppers.

She'd nearly killed someone. Inadvertently, maybe, but the shame and the guilt were still hers to bear.

Gina gazed at Morgan, forcing herself to smile. "So, who asked about me?"

"Flint Kingman."

Her smile cracked and fell. "He's here?"

"Yes. He asked me to point you out."

"Did he?" Gina glanced around the room. The crème de la crème of Boston society mingled freely, but somewhere, lurking amid black cocktail dresses and designer suits, was her newly acquired rival.

Anxious, she fingered the diamond-and-pearl choker around her neck, wishing she hadn't worn it. Flint's reputation strangled her like a noose.

The wonder boy. The renowned spin doctor. The prince of the PR world.

Her family expected her to work with him, to take his advice. Why couldn't they allow her the dignity of repairing the media damage on her own? Why did they have to force Flint Kingman on her?

He'd left a slew of messages at the office, insisting she return his calls. So finally she'd summoned the strength to do just that. But their professional conversation had turned heated, and she'd told him to go to hell.

And now he was here.

"Would you mind pointing him out to me?" she asked Morgan.

"Certainly." The redhead turned to glance over her shoulder, then frowned. "He was over there, with that group of men, but he's gone now."

Gina shrugged, hoping to appear calm and refined—a far cry from the turmoil churning inside.

"I'm sure he'll catch up with me later," she said, wondering if he'd attended this party just to intimidate her.

If he didn't crawl out of the woodwork and introduce himself, then he would probably continue to spy on her from afar, making her ulcer act up. It was a nervous condition she hid from her family.

"If you'll excuse me, Morgan, I'm going to check out the buffet."

"Go right ahead. If I see Flint, I'll let you know."

"Thanks." Gina headed to the buffet table to indulge in hors d'oeuvres, to nibble daintily on party foods, to pretend that she felt secure enough to eat in public. No way would she let Flint run her off, even if she wanted to dart out the door.

As she studied the festive spread, her stomach tightened. This wasn't the bland diet her doctor recommended, but what choice did she have?

The shrimp dumplings would probably hit her digestive

system like lead balls, but she placed them on her plate next to a scatter of crab-stuffed mushrooms and a small helping of artichoke dip.

Balancing her food and a full glass of wine, she searched for a sheltered spot. The posh hotel banquet room had been decorated for a cocktail gathering with a small grouping of tables and lots of standing room.

Gina snuggled up to a floor-to-ceiling window, set her drink on a nearby planter ledge and turned to gaze at the city. Rain fell from the sky, and lights twinkled like pinwheels, casting sparks in the brisk March air.

She stood, with her plate in hand, admiring the rain-dampened view. And then she heard a man speak her name.

The low, vodka-on-the-rocks voice crept up her spine and sent her heartbeat racing. She recognized Flint Kingman's tone instantly.

Preparing to face him, she turned.

He gazed directly into her eyes, and she did her damnedest to maintain her composure.

She'd expected tall and handsome, but he was more than that. So much more.

In an Armani suit and Gucci loafers, he stood perfectly groomed, as cocky and debonair as his reputation. Yet beneath the Boston polish was an edge as hard as his name, as sharp and dangerous as the tip of a flint.

He exuded sexuality. Pure, raw, primal heat.

She steadied her plate with both hands to keep her food from spilling onto the floor. Men didn't make her nervous. But this one did.

He didn't speak; he just watched her through a pair of amber-flecked eyes.

"Aren't you going to introduce yourself?" she said, her posture stiff, her fingers suddenly numb.

A cynical smile tugged at the corner of his lips, and a strand of chocolate-brown hair fell rebelliously across his forehead.

"Nice try. But you know exactly who I am."

"Oh, forgive me. You must be that Bowie guy."

He smoothed his hair into place, his mouth still set in a sardonic curl. "Flint. Bowie is a different kind of knife."

And both would cut just as sharp, she thought, just as brutal.

Like a self-assured predator, he moved a little closer, just enough to put his pheromones between them. She took a deep breath, and the sore in her stomach ignited into a red-hot flame.

Damn her nerves, she thought. And damn him.

"I'll stop by your office on Tuesday," he said. "At two."

"I'll check my calendar and get back to you," she countered, wishing she could dig through her purse for an antacid.

He shook his head. "Tuesday at two. This isn't up for negotiation."

Gina bristled, hating Flint Kingman and everything he represented. Would the stress ever end? The guilt? The professional humiliation? "Are you always this pushy?"

"I'm aggressive, not pushy."

"You could have fooled me."

She lifted her chin a notch, and Flint studied the stubborn gesture. Gina Barone was a feminine force to be reckoned with—a long, elegant body, a mass of wavy brown hair swept into a proper chignon and eyes the color of violets.

A cold shoulder and a hot temper. He'd heard she was an ice princess. A woman much too defensive. A woman who competed with men. And now she would be competing with him.

She gave him an annoyed look, and he glanced at her untouched hors d'oeuvres. "Don't you like the food?"

"I haven't had the chance to eat it."

"Why? Because I interrupted you?" He reached out, snagged a mushroom off her plate and popped it into his mouth, knowing damn well his blatant behavior would rile her even further.

Those violet eyes turned a little violent, and he suspected she was contemplating a childish act, like flinging the rest of the mushrooms at him. He pictured them hitting his chest like crab-stuffed bullets. "I don't have cooties, Miss Barone."

"You don't have any manners, either."

"Of course I do." He went after a dumpling this time, ate it with relish, then reached into his jacket for a monogrammed handkerchief and wiped his hands with casual elegance. This party was too damn prissy, he thought. And so was Gina Barone. Flint was sick to death of the superficial society in which he lived. He used to thrive on this world, but now it seemed like a lie.

Then again, why wouldn't it? After all, he'd just uncovered a family secret, a skeleton in his closet that made his entire life seem like a lie.

Still eyeing him with disdain, Gina set her plate on the planter ledge. "Thanks to you, I lost my appetite."

She didn't have one to begin with, he thought. The trouble at Baronessa Gelati must be weighing heavily on her inexperienced shoulders. She'd never outfoxed a public scandal, particularly something of this magnitude.

Flint had, of course. Scandals were his specialty. But not family secrets. He couldn't outfox the lie in which he'd been raised.

He dragged a hand through his hair and then realized that he'd zoned out, losing sight of his priority. Nothing, not even the turmoil in his life, should interfere with business.

Pulling himself into the moment, he stared at Gina.

Did she resent his take-charge attitude? Or did the truth upset her? The fact that he was more qualified for the job?

Truthfully, he didn't care. He was damn good at what he did and he'd worked hard to prove his worth.

"Stop looking at me like that," she said.

"Like what?"

"Like you're superior."

"Men are superior," he responded, deliberately baiting her.

"And that's why Adam ate the apple?" she asked. "Because he had brains?"

"What kind of question is that?"

She rolled her eyes. "A rhetorical one. Everyone knows Adam ate the apple because of Eve."

Which meant what? That she thought the male brain hinged on what was behind his zipper? Or in Adam's case, a fig leaf?

Flint assessed his companion. The lights from the city shimmered behind her, as white and bright as the diamond brooch on the front of her choker. It was an exceptional piece, but he would have preferred an unadorned view of her neck. She had smooth, touchable skin, kissed by the sun and boasting her Sicilian roots.

His gaze slipped slower, to the swell of her breasts. No matter how high a man's IQ was, his brain did get scrambled now and then. Flint was no exception.

He lifted his gaze. "I'm not offended, Miss Barone."

"About what?"

"About you thinking my brain is in my pants."

"Well, you should be."

"And you should offer me a shiny red apple." He paused for effect. "I'll take a big, juicy bite if you will."

Gina glared at him.

Enjoying the game, he flashed a flirtatious smile. Sparring with her was actually kind of fun. And it certainly beat crying into his beer.

"I'll be damned if I'm going to work with you," she said.

He tilted his head, wondering what she would look like

with her hair rioting around her face, framing her in untamed glory. "As I understand it, you don't have a choice."

"Don't bet on it," she quipped.

"I'll see you on Tuesday. At two o'clock," he reminded her before he walked away.

His lovely nemesis was quite a challenge. But he wasn't worried about it. Sooner or later, she'd give in and let him fix the disaster in her life.

Even if he couldn't fix his own.

Gina awakened with a start the following morning. She sat up and squinted, then hugged a pillow to her chest.

She'd actually dreamed about Flint Kingman.

And erotic dream. An illusion of mist and midnight, of his long, lean, muscled torso gleaming in the rain.

While she'd slept through a stormy night, he'd invaded her bedroom, her private sanctuary.

Gina reached for her robe and wrapped herself in terry cloth. Everything seemed different now. The cherry armoire and big brass bed. The hardwood floors and Turkish rugs.

With a deep breath, she turned and peered out the blinds. Thank God, it wasn't raining anymore. She never wanted it to rain again. Not if it meant revisiting that half-naked image of Flint, his head tipped back, water running in rivulets down his stomach and into the waistband of slim black trousers.

Gina tightened her robe. She'd dreamed of him in the clothes he'd worn last night, only he'd been standing on the rooftop of the hotel, allowing her to undress him.

Damn that sexy smile of his. And damn that cocky attitude.

She had two days before their meeting, two days to arm herself with information. She knew virtually nothing about Flint, but she suspected he knew plenty about her.

He'd probably done his homework weeks ago, analyzing

his opponent, charting her strengths and weaknesses, her successes, her failures.

Well, at least her dreams were her own. And so was her ulcer. She doubted Flint had pried into her medical records.

She crossed the living room, entered the kitchen and eyed the coffeepot. It sat on a bright, white counter, luring her with the temptation of a hard, strong dose of caffeine.

With a practical sigh, she poured herself a glass of milk instead, then reached for the phone.

Seated at the breakfast nook, she looked up Morgan Chancellor's number, hoping the socialite was available. Morgan wasn't a vicious gossip. She didn't spread unholy rumors, but she seemed to know everybody's business. And Gina intended to discuss Flint with someone willing to answer questions about him.

Morgan picked up on the fifth ring. Gina started a friendly conversation, asking the other woman if she'd enjoyed the charity mixer.

Morgan babbled for a while, and Gina pictured the redhead's no-nonsense husband scanning the *Boston Globe* at their elegant dining room table, shutting out his wife's perky voice.

Weaving her way toward the man of the hour, Gina said, "By the way, Flint Kingman finally caught up with me."

"Really? So, what do you think of him?"

Gina shoved away the image of his dream-induced, rain-shrouded body. "I'm not sure. I can't quite figure him out." When the other woman breathed into the receiver, she asked, "What do you know about him, Morgan?"

"Hmm. Let's see. His father is an advertising mogul, and his stepmother is absolutely riveting. Of course his real mother was equally stunning. She was a Hollywood starlet, but she died when Flint was a baby."

Intrigued, Gina adjusted the phone. "Was she famous?"

"No, but she should have been. Supposedly she was really talented."

Gina tried to picture the woman who'd given Flint King-man life. "What was her name?"

"Danielle Wolf. But there isn't a lot of old press about her. If you're really curious about Flint, you should read up on Tara Shaw."

"The movie star?" The aging bombshell? The world-famous blonde? "Why? Was she friends with his mother?"

Morgan made a crunching sound, as if she were eating breakfast while she talked. "Oh, no. It's nothing like that. Flint used to work for Tara."

"So? He's a PR consultant. That's perfectly understand-able."

The crunching sound stopped. "He had an affair with her, Gina."

"Oh, my goodness." Flint and Tara Shaw? The screen goddess of the 1970s? She had to be twice his age.

Morgan resumed eating. "Some reports say she broke his heart. Others say he broke hers. And some say they were both just playing around, tearing up the sheets for the fun of it."

Gina shifted in her seat, nearly spilling her milk. She grabbed the glass before it tipped over. "When did this happen?"

"When he was fresh out of college. I'm surprised you didn't hear about it."

"Normally, I don't pay attention to things like that. I've never really followed the Hollywood scene."

"Well, I do," Morgan said. "Their affair didn't last long, but it created quite a scandal."

"Bigger than the one going on in my life?"

"Much bigger."

That was all it took. Gina spent the rest of the morning on the Internet, pulling up old articles on Tara Shaw and her wild, young lover.

While driving past the prestigious homes in Beacon Hill, Flint got the sudden urge to call Tara, to tell her what was going on.

He glanced at his car phone and realized foolishly that he didn't have her number. He hadn't spoken to Tara Shaw in over eight years. Flint had left Hollywood without looking back.

Besides, what the hell would he say to her? And what would her new husband think if her old lover just happened to ring her up?

With a squeal of his tires, he turned onto a familiar street and pulled into his parents' driveway, knowing his dad would be home on a Sunday afternoon.

Flint and his father saw each other often. They worked in the same bustling high-rise, but these days they rarely spoke, at least not about important issues.

He unlocked the door with his key, the same key he'd had since he was a teenager. For eighteen years, this elegant mansion had been his home.

He stood in the marbled foyer for a moment, catching his reflection in a beveled mirror. It wasn't a cold house, completely void of emotion, but it didn't present a warm, fuzzy feeling, either.

But then how could it? Especially now?

He crossed the salon, passing Chippendale settees, ornate tables and gilded statues. The Kingmans were a successful family, but money didn't necessarily make people happy.

He located his dad in the garden room, a timber and-glass structure flourishing with greenery. Shimmering vines twined around redwood trellises, and colorful buds bloomed in a shower of floral abundance, thriving in the controlled environment.

James Kingman, a tall, serious man, with a square jaw

and wide shoulders, enjoyed growing flowers, and he tended them with a gentle hand.

Today he hovered over a cluster of lady's slippers, orchids as beautiful and beguiling as their fairy-tale name.

Flint shed his jacket, and the older man looked up.

"Well, hello," he said, acknowledging his son's presence. "What brings you by?"

You, me and my mom, he thought. *The past, the present, the pain.* "I was hoping we could talk."

"About what?"

"My mother."

James shook head. "I don't want to rehash all of that again."

"But I want to talk about it."

"There's nothing more to talk about. I told you everything. Just forget about it, let it go."

Let it go? Forget about it?

Two weeks ago Flint had stumbled upon a horrible secret, and now the truth haunted him like a ghost. "You lied to me all those years, Dad."

James shifted his stance. He wore jeans and a denim shirt, but he was impeccably groomed—a man of wealth and taste. "I did it to protect you. Why won't you accept that?"

"Just tell me this much. Does *Nĭsh'kĭ* know the truth?" he asked, thinking about his Cheyenne grandmother.

"Yes, she knew when it happened. It broke her heart."

And now it's breaking mine, Flint thought.

"You can't bring this up to your grandmother," his dad said. "It wouldn't be right."

Flint nodded. As a rule, the Cheyenne didn't speak freely of the dead, and *Nĭsh'kĭ* adhered to the old way. "Is she aware that I came upon the truth?"

"Yes, I told her. But she didn't want to discuss it."

No one wanted to discuss it, no one but Flint. Didn't they understand that he needed to grieve? To come to terms with his role in all of this?

"It isn't fair," he said.

"Life isn't fair," James replied, using a cliché that only made Flint feel worse.

In the next instant they both fell silent. Water trickled from an ornamental fountain, mimicking the patter of rain.

Flint glanced at the glass ceiling and noticed dark clouds floating across a hazy blue sky.

He shrugged into his jacket. "I better go. I've got things to do."

James met his troubled gaze. "Don't be angry, son."

Flint looked at his dad, at the blond hair turning a silvery shade of gray. He'd inherited his dad's hazel eyes, but his dark hair and copper skin had come from his mother. The woman he wasn't allowed to talk about.

"I'm not," he said. It wasn't anger eating away at his soul. It was pain. "I'll see you tomorrow at the office. Give Faith a kiss for me," he added, referring to his stepmother.

"She'll be sorry she missed you."

"I know." He loved Faith Kingman. She'd raised him since he was ten years old, but she wasn't willing to talk about this, either. Not if it meant betraying her husband.

Flint left his parents' house, and James went back to his flowers, hiding behind their vibrant colors and velvet petals.

On Tuesday, Gina wore what she considered a power suit to the office. The blouse matched her eyes, the tailored black jacket nipped at her waist and the slim-fitting skirt rode just above her knees. But her pumps, bless them, were her secret weapon. When she strode through Baronessa's corporate halls, they made a determined, confident click, giving her an air of feminine authority.

The fourth floor of the chrome-and-glass structure was Gina's domain, and she often gazed out the windows, drawing strength from the city.

Today she needed all she could get.

She glanced at the clock on the wall. Flint would be here any minute.

Gina moved in front of her desk and remained standing, waiting anxiously for his arrival. She'd been rehearsing this moment in her mind for two days, practicing her lines, her gestures.

She knew plenty about Flint Kingman now. She'd even uncovered a few facts about his mother. Danielle Wolf, a half-Indian beauty from the Cheyenne reservation, had left home to pursue an acting career. Five years later she'd abandoned Hollywood to become a wife and mother and then died in a car accident a month after her son was born.

Gina intended to rent the B movies Danielle had co-starred in. She suspected Flint had inherited his mother's adventurous spirit. It wouldn't hurt to analyze every aspect of her opponent's personality, particularly if she was going to kick him off this harrowing project.

Gina's secretary buzzed. She pressed the intercom. "Yes?"

"Mr. Kingman is here."

She let out the breath she'd been holding. "Send him in."

A minute later he strode through the door in a gray suit and silver-gray tie, his thick dark hair combed away from his face. Suddenly Gina could see the Native American in him—the rich color of his skin, the killer cheekbones, the deep-set eyes. They looked more brown than gold today, and she realized they were actually a stunning, ever-changing shade of hazel.

He flashed a cocky grin, and she reached for the apple

on her desk and tossed it to him. Or at him, she supposed, since she'd heaved it like a shiny red baseball.

Caught off guard, he fumbled, dropped his briefcase and retrieved the apple in the nick of time.

The grin returned to his lips. "The forbidden fruit, Miss Barone?"

"Consider it a parting gift."

He arched an eyebrow. "Am I going somewhere?"

"Anywhere but here," she said, leaning against her desk like a corporate vamp. "I told you before that I'm not working with you."

He picked up his briefcase and came forward. As self-assured as ever, he pulled up a chair and sat down, studying the apple.

"What are you doing?" she asked.

"Checking for worms."

She smiled in spite of herself. "I'm not that evil."

He lifted his gaze, and her smile fell. Why did he have to look at her like that? So sly, so sexy. She could almost feel his rain-slicked, dream-induced skin.

"All women are evil. And beautiful and clever in their own way," he said. "I enjoy females."

"So I've heard." She walked around to the other side of her desk and sank into her leather chair, hoping to appear more powerful than she felt.

"You're holding my dating record against me?" he asked.

"You mean your scorecard? Let's face it, Mr. Kingman. You're a player. You drive a fast, ferocious, racy red Corvette, keep company with bimbos and then notch your bedpost after each insensitive conquest."

He gave her a level stare. "Nice try, but that's not quite accurate. You see, I have a brass bed, and the metal is a little hard to notch."

Gina steeled her nerves. She had a brass bed, too. The one he'd invaded. ''You indulged in an affair with a movie star twice your age.''

Something flashed in his eyes. Pain? Anger? Male pride? She couldn't be sure.

''Aren't you going to defend yourself?'' she asked, confused by his silence.

Suddenly Flint Kingman, the confident, carefree spin doctor, was impossible to read.

Two

___

Gina waited for him to respond, but he just sat there, staring at her.

"Well?" she asked, unnerved by those unwavering eyes.

Finally he blinked, sending sparks of amber shooting through his irises. "What do you want me to say? I was only twenty-two at the time."

Which meant what? That he'd actually been in love? Or that he'd been too young and too wild to control his sexual urges?

"How are you going to polish Baronessa's reputation when your own reputation isn't exactly glowing?" she asked, refusing to let it go. Flint had been a virile twenty-two-year-old, and Tara had been a dazzling role model for forty-three-year-olds everywhere, proving women could be desirable at any age. But their relationship still bothered Gina.

He squared his shoulders. "I'm more than qualified to pull Baronessa out of this mess."

"And so am I." Even if she had been the one who'd unwittingly dragged Baronessa into it.

"Really?" He placed his briefcase on his lap and opened it, and with the flick of his wrists he scattered a stack of supermarket tabloids across Gina's desk.

The headlines hit her square in the chest.

Mysterious Curse Destroys Ice Cream Empire.

Mafia Mayhem in Boston. Will the Sicilian-Born Barones Survive?

Passion Fruit Versus Passion Death. Who Tried to Murder an Innocent Man?

"I've read these," she said. "And they're filled with lies. That curse is nonsense. My family isn't connected to the mob. And the man who suffered an allergic reaction to the peppers recovered with no ill effects."

"Maybe so, but just stating the facts isn't enough. What's your plan to counter the negative press, Miss Barone? This is some pretty heavy-duty stuff."

She shoved the tabloids aside, and her ulcer sprang to life, her stomach acids eating a hole right through her, creating a familiar pain.

"I intend to hold a contest," she said. "Something that will get the public involved."

"Like what? Name That Curse?"

Smart-ass, she thought, narrowing her eyes at him. "More like create a new gelato flavor. Baronessa will invite the public to come up with a flavor to replace passionfruit. The winner of the contest and the new flavor will get lots of press, plenty of positive media attention."

He sat quietly, mulling over her idea. Finally he said, "That's a great marketing tool, but it's too soon for a contest. First we need something juicier. A bigger scandal, something that will make the press forget all about that pepper fiasco."

"And I suppose you've already cooked up the perfect scandal."

He smoothed his hair, a gesture she'd seen more than once. But he did have that rebellious strand, the Elvis lock that repeatedly fell forward.

"Truthfully," he admitted, "I haven't zeroed in on the perfect scandal, but when I do, you'll be the first to know."

"I don't like the idea," she told him. "All we'll be doing is replacing one set of lies for another. That doesn't cut it for me."

"Too bad. It's the way to go. Believe me, I've worked this angle before." He reached for one of the tabloids. "So what's the deal on this curse?"

Gina pressed against the pain, the gnawing, burning sensation in her stomach. "Aren't you supposed to know all of this already?"

"I want to hear it in your words. I want your take on the curse."

"I already told you, it's nonsense." She rose and walked to the bar. Not because she was a gracious hostess, but because she needed to coat the burn. "Would you like something to drink?" she asked.

He shook his head, and she poured herself a glass of milk. "It does a body good," she said, when he eyed the white liquid curiously.

He roamed his gaze over her, sweeping her curves with masculine appreciation. "So I see."

Her pulse shot up her arm. *Don't flirt with me,* she thought. *Don't look at me with those bedroom eyes.*

But he did. He watched her. Closely. They way he'd watched her in that dream, just seconds before she'd undressed him.

Neither spoke. They stared at each other, caught in one those awkward, sexually stirring moments.

Finally, he broke eye contact, and she brought the milk to her lips. The thick, creamy drink slid down her throat.

"The curse," Flint reminded her, his voice a little too rough.

Gina took her seat, struggling for composure. This felt like a curse, she thought. This impossible attraction.

"It started with my grandfather," she said. "He jilted a girl who'd wanted to marry him, and on Valentine's Day, he eloped with my grandmother instead. So the other girl put a curse on my grandparents and their descendants. She vowed that misery would strike on their anniversary, marking Valentine's Day a holiday of disaster."

"Then why did you schedule the passionfruit tasting on February fourteenth?" he asked. "That seems a little risky to me."

"Because I was determined to prove that curse wrong. Besides, a flavor called passionfruit made a nice Valentine's Day promotion." She drank some more milk. "Or it should have."

He gathered the tabloids and put them into his briefcase. "You lied to me, Miss Barone. You don't think the curse is nonsense. You believe in it now."

Steeped in guilt, she defended herself. "I'm not a superstitious woman, but I should have been more cautious. Some unfortunate things have happened to my family on Valentine's Day over the years, but those events seemed like coincidence. A fluke here and there."

"Don't worry about it," he said. "I'll repair the damage."

"No, I will," she countered.

He shrugged, then taunted her with that slow, sensual smile, reminding her that she'd dreamed about him.

When he stood to leave, she heard a sudden burst of rain hit the windows behind her.

A cool, hard, male-driven rain.

After Flint departed, Gina went straight to her brother's office. Nicholas held the prestigious COO title, the chief operations officer, at Baronessa Gelati.

He stood well over six feet, with a strong, athletic build,

jet-black hair and blue eyes. Women, including his new wife and daughter, found him irresistible. Gina, however, considered herself immune to his charm. He'd abandoned his playboy ways for a blissful marriage, but he still had a high dose of testosterone running through his veins, which made him difficult to manipulate.

"I want you to fire Flint Kingman," she said.

Nicholas sat behind his desk and rolled his impressive shoulders, looking like the powerful corporate male he was. "Why?"

Because I dreamed about him, she wanted to say. *He invaded my mind, my bed.* "Because he's going to do this company more harm than good."

"How so?"

"He intends to cook up a phony scandal to divert the press."

"That's what he does, Gina. He's a spin doctor and a damn good one. I trust his instincts."

"What about my instincts?"

"You're a bright, capable woman, but this is his area of expertise."

She sat across from her brother and picked up a rubber band off his desk, wishing she could flick it at him. He was eight years her senior, and he'd always treated her like a child. He used to call her noodle head because curls sprang from her scalp like spiral pasta.

Gina glared at Nicholas and smoothed her hair. These days she tamed her curls in a professional chignon. "So you're taking Flint's side?"

He leaned forward, trapping her gaze. "His side? You're not turning this into a gender war, are you?"

She thought about the apple, the forbidden fruit, she'd tossed at Flint this afternoon. "He bosses me around."

"Probably because you're fighting him every step of the way. You've got to curb your temper, Gina."

She stretched the rubber band, wishing she had the courage to let it fly.

"We brought Flint in as a consultant." Nicholas went on. "The idea is for the two of you to work together."

"Fine." She could see this was going nowhere. Coming to her feet, she blew a frustrated breath. Rain still pounded against the windows, reminding her that Flint controlled the weather, too.

Would she ever get that image out of her mind? That long, lean, water-slicked body?

"And don't go running to Dad about this," Nicholas warned.

"I don't intend to," she responded, trying to sound more grown-up than she felt. "I'll work with Flint if I have to. But I won't let him call all the shots."

Nicholas grinned. "Spoken like a true woman."

"And don't you forget it." She turned to march out of his office, her feminine armor—the tailored suit and high-heeled pumps—securely in place.

"I love you, noodle head," he said before she reached the door.

She stopped and smiled. She loved Nicholas Barone, too. Even if he was her big, brawny, know-it-all brother.

Hours later Gina drove home, her windshield wipers clapping to the rhythm of the rain. She lived in a brownstone in the North End, a family-owned, renovated building she shared with two of her sisters. They each had their own sprawling apartment, but they often gathered in the community living room on the first floor to curl up with a bowl of extra-buttered popcorn and talk.

She parked her car and walked to the front of the brownstone, only to find Flint sitting on the stoop, his overcoat flapping in the wind.

She stopped dead in her tracks and stared at him. He looked up, his face speckled with rain, his waterlogged hair slick and shiny.

"It didn't work, did it?" he said.

"Excuse me?"

"Your brother wouldn't fire me, would he?"

She moved forward, taking shelter from the storm. How did he know that she'd complained to Nicholas? Was she that predictable?

He rose, attacking her with that insufferable smile. "I want you to have dinner with me tonight."

Her heart pole-vaulted its way to her throat. "What? Why?"

"So we can get used to each other. We've got a lot of work ahead of us. And there's no point in wasting time."

She snuggled deeper into her coat. "But it's raining."

He gave her an odd look. "You don't eat when it rains?"

Of course, she did. She just didn't relish the idea of spending time in his company, particularly with water falling from the sky.

Then again, maybe a business dinner would take the edge off. Maybe it would help her forget that other image. "Fine. I'll have a meal with you." But he'd better not steal food from her plate, she thought.

"Meet me at the Beef and Bull around seven," he said. It's a steak house on—"

"I know where it is," she interrupted. "And I'll be there at eight."

"Seven-thirty," he challenged.

"Eight," she countered in a firm tone. She needed time to bathe, to change, to fix her rain-drizzled hair.

"All right," he said, giving in with a grumble. "But don't be late."

Gina reached for her keys and sent him a triumphant smile. She'd finally gotten her way. On a small scale, maybe, but it was a start.

At precisely eight o'clock, Flint arrived at the Beef and Bull, a quiet, dimly lit steak house decorated with knotty-pine walls and Western antiques.

He approached the hostess and gave her his name. "I'm expecting a companion," he said. "Has she arrived yet?"

The young woman shook her head. "No, Mr. Kingman, she hasn't."

He gestured to a shadowy corner in the waiting room. "I'll just kick back over there until she gets here."

The hostess nodded and smiled. He returned her polite smile and moved out of the way, giving the people behind him a chance to check their reservation.

Settling onto a leather cushion, he stretched his legs out in front of him.

Impatient, he checked his watch, and suddenly the diamond-and-gold timepiece glinted like a superficial jewel, a reminder of who he was and where he'd come from.

Damn it, he thought. Why couldn't he accept the way things were? The way he'd been raised?

Because his charmed life had changed. Flint Kingman wasn't the same man anymore. The truth about his mother had altered his heart, his soul, the very core of his existence.

Gina entered the restaurant, and he steadied his emotions.

No matter how troubled he was, he wouldn't let it affect his career. The Barones had hired him to defuse the crisis in their company. And come hell or high water, that was what he intended to do.

He remained seated and assessed Gina for a moment. After he'd left her office this afternoon, he'd come up with a plan. A damn good one. But it meant getting close to Gina, not close enough to infringe on the confused order of his life, but close enough to fool the public.

And with that in mind, he'd invited her to dinner. He needed to see her in a romantic setting, to explore the energy between them.

The sexual energy, he thought. The unexpected heat.

Gina Barone couldn't stand his dominating personality,

and her high-and-mighty attitude annoyed the hell out of him. But that didn't matter. This was strictly business, a teeth-gnashing, tough-to-temper attraction that could work in their favor.

Besides, he'd already fantasized about her. Earlier this evening, when he'd taken a stress-relieving shower, she'd slipped right into the steam.

He hadn't meant to think about her and certainly not in a state of undress, but he'd lost the battle. With a sizzling, soap-scented mirage of her in his mind, he couldn't seem to control the yearning, the I'm-too-old-for-wet-dreams hunger. Trapped beneath a spray of warm water, he'd closed his eyes and imagined her—

She turned and saw him, and Flint gulped a gust of air.

How tall was she? he wondered. Five-nine? Five-ten? In his mind's eye, she'd fit him perfectly in the shower, that sweet, slim, incredibly moist body—

She moved closer, and he came to his feet, his six-foot-three frame still draped in a knee-length raincoat. Beneath it, he wore a suit with a Western flair, but if he didn't get his hormones in check, he would be sporting a big, boyish bulge in the vicinity of his zipper.

"You're late," he told her, when they were eye to eye.

"And you're acting like a jerk, as usual," she responded.

He couldn't help but smile. They had the weirdest chemistry, but somehow it worked.

Of course that ice-princess act of hers wouldn't charm the media, and it wouldn't seduce the public, either. Which meant he would have to revamp her image a little.

She removed her coat, and he slid his gaze up and down the luscious length of her body. Oh, yeah, he thought. He could mold her into a nice yet naughty girl—a kitten with a whip.

"What are you doing?" she asked.

"Just looking," he responded, shooting a smile straight

into her eyes. Her dress wasn't quite short enough, but the creamy beige color complemented her skin.

He reached out to loosen one of her curls, but she backed away, refusing to let him touch her. "Keep your hands to yourself, Kingman."

"But the rain messed up your hair," he lied. "I was just going to fix it."

She huffed out a shallow breath, and he knew he'd made her nervous. A good kind of nervous. The sexy kind.

"My hair's fine," she said.

No, it wasn't, he thought, itching to tousle it. The lady-of-the-manor style was too damn proper, too coiffed.

"Are you going to buy me dinner or not?" she asked.

"Sure. Let's get our table."

The hostess seated them in a fairly secluded booth. A snow-white candle dripped wax, and a single red rose bloomed in a bud vase, giving the rustic tabletop a touch of date-night ambience.

The waiter came by, offering cocktails. Gina declined a glass of wine, opting for iced tea instead. Flint went for an imported beer.

Silent, they studied their menus. Five minutes later, when the waiter returned with their drinks, Flint and Gina ordered the same meal. Or nearly the same meal, with the exception of a rare steak for him and a well-done cut for her.

Soon a basket of warm bread arrived. He reached out to offer her a slice at the same time she chose to get one for herself. But before their hands collided, she pulled back.

He took the lead, following his original plan. Tilting the basket toward her, he said, "Go ahead, Miss Barone. Or would it be all right if I called you Gina?"

She made her selection, then proceeded to lather it with whipped butter. "Gina is fine."

He watched her take a bite. "And so is Flint," he told her.

She swallowed and then made a pleasured sound, like a soft, sweet, bedroom murmur.

Amused, he reached for his beer. "Say it," he said.

She glanced up. "Excuse me?"

"My name. Say my name."

She gave him a curious look. "Flint."

Enjoying himself, he bit back a grin. "That was pretty good, but it wasn't quite right. You need to moan after you say my name, like you did after you ate the bread."

Finally aware of his little joke, she shoved the basket toward him. "Stuff it, *Flint*."

He flashed the grin he'd been hiding. "I couldn't help it. I mean, here's a woman who gets orgasmic over bread and butter."

"I wasn't orgasmic."

"Yes, you were."

"I was not."

She glared at him from across the table, but her haughty expression fell short. When he stared at her, she became flustered, toying with the napkin on her lap.

"Don't," she said.

"Don't what?"

"Look at me like that."

He studied her features, struck by those violet eyes and that full, lush mouth. "But you're beautiful, Gina." And he couldn't stop the attraction, the heat, the sexual spontaneity rising in his blood.

She drew a ragged breath, and a shimmer of silence ensued.

Rain pounded against the building, and the flame on the candle danced between them, intensifying the moment.

Flint sent her a small, sensual smile. She was perfect for the scandal he had in mind.

Three

——

Two days later Gina entered the impressive high-rise that housed Kingman Marketing, a global advertising, public-relations and marketing agency.

Flint had called her this morning, demanding a meeting. Gina had tried to talk him into coming to her office, but he'd refused. For some unexplained reason, he wanted her on his turf.

She suspected that he'd devised a scandal and intended to make a presentation of some sort.

Standing in front of the elevator, she waited for the doors to open. She'd done some research on Kingman Marketing and learned that the company had built its stellar reputation on a high-profile clientele, which included well-known corporations, politicians and celebrities.

Like Tara Shaw, she thought. The actress Flint had bedded all those years ago.

The elevator opened, and Gina entered the confined space. Alone with her thoughts, she pressed the appropriate button and released an edgy breath. She wasn't comfortable seeing Flint again, especially after that awkward "business" dinner.

They'd stared at each other half the night like sex-starved teenagers on a first date. She'd hated every minute of that warm, woozy, he's-so-gorgeous feeling. She'd struggled through the meal, the food melting in her mouth like an unwelcome aphrodisiac. And he kept smiling at her, teasing her in that playful manner of his, which had only managed to make her more nervous.

The elevator stopped, and Gina stepped into the hallway and faced a set of smoked-glass doors, knowing it was the entrance to Flint's domain.

The sixth floor was dedicated to the public-relations department, and she'd heard that he ran his division with strength, strategy and creativity.

She stalled for a moment, battling a bout of anxiety. Smoothing her jacket, she told herself to relax. She didn't intend to let Flint eye her the way he'd done at the restaurant. Today she wore a camel-colored pantsuit, a ribbed turtleneck and conservative boots. Aside from her hands and face, she was completely covered. This outfit couldn't possibly turn him on.

Ready to do battle, she went inside, and then she stood and gazed around the massive reception area.

Antiques from every corner of the world made an incredible display, and so did modern works of art. She knew instantly that Flint had worked closely with the decorator.

"Are you Gina Barone?"

She turned to see a slim, chic woman rise from a birch desk—a unique piece of furniture that fit her vogue style. Alabaster skin showcased cropped black hair and trendy black glasses, making her look fashionably efficient.

"Yes, I am."

The woman came forward and extended her hand. "I'm Kerry Landau, Flint's assistant."

Gina smiled. "It's nice to meet you."

Kerry lowered her glasses and peered at Gina with exotically lined eyes. "I couldn't help but notice that you were admiring the decor." She pointed to a table-high statue—a depiction of a long, lean, naked lady. "That's my husband's work. He's still a struggling artist. But he's exceptional."

"Yes, he is." Gina studied the piece. The marble lady stood there, one hand draped between her thighs, her other arm barely shielding her aroused nipples. She seemed sensuously vulnerable, innocent yet erotic.

Gina turned to speak to Kerry and caught sight of Flint. He'd appeared out of nowhere, and he leaned against the doorjamb that led to his office, his head tilted at a curious angle.

"Ms. Barone is here," Kerry announced.

"So I see."

Flint's gaze roamed over Gina's carefully clothed body, and suddenly she felt as naked as the statue. And just as vulnerable.

"Are you ready?" he asked.

To enter the wolf's private den? No, she wasn't the least bit ready. "Of course."

"Good." He escorted her down a brightly lit hallway and into his office.

Offering her a seat, he gestured to a comfortable yet elegant sitting area. He'd spared no expense in decorating his domain, and she suspected his family was as wealthy as hers. But that was where the similarity ended.

Flint was an only child—the prince, the heir to the Kingman throne. Gina, on the other hand, struggled with being a middle child, the one her parents overlooked, the one who had to work twice as hard to get noticed.

Gina sighed, then glanced up and caught Flint watching her.

Uncomfortable, she folded her hands on her lap.

He moved to stand in front of his desk—a rich, intricately carved block of mahogany.

"You have exceptional taste," she said, struggling to fill the silence.

A small smile curved his lips. "In women?"

She shifted on the sofa. "In furniture."

"Thank you." The teasing smile remained. "Would you like a drink? Coffee, tea, a soft drink?" He walked to the bar. "A glass of milk?"

"A cup of hot tea would be nice," she responded, wishing he would stop flirting.

"Coming right up."

Within minutes he placed a silver tea set on the table beside her. It looked much too refined to be served by a tall, broad-shouldered man.

He sat across from her, looking wildly attractive, his rebellious hair falling onto his forehead.

She prepared her tea, adding cream and sugar. "So, what's the purpose of this meeting? Did you mastermind a scandal?"

"Yes."

She tasted the hot brew, sipping delicately. "And?"

"And I think we should have an affair."

Gina nearly spilled her tea, and Flint laughed.

"Not a real affair," he clarified.

"Let me get this straight." She set her cup on the table, knowing she wasn't steady enough to balance it. Apparently he'd meant to knock her for a loop, to heave his proposal at her, much in the way she'd tossed that apple at him. "You're suggesting we fake an affair?"

"That's right. A whirlwind romance and a stormy breakup."

She released a choppy breath. "You can't be serious."

"Of course, I am. Your family is already being targeted in the tabloids, so you'll draw plenty of attention. And so will I, considering I've been in the spotlight before."

Yes, he'd been in the spotlight before, playing around with a movie star.

"I'm telling you. This will work. Just picture the headlines. 'PR prince melts Italian ice-cream princess.' It'll make great copy."

She shook her head, still trying to fathom the idea. "We don't even like each other."

"So what? It's just a phony affair. Three weeks of prominent dating, then a public breakup, and I'll be out of your hair." He removed his jacket and loosened his tie, giving himself a rakish look. "By the time we're done with the media, they won't care about pepper-spiced gelato or family curses. All they'll care about is the hip-grinding, mind-blowing displays of affection we'll be tossing their way." He gazed directly into her eyes. "Come on, what do you have to lose?"

My sanity, she thought.

"We've got great chemistry, Gina." He moved onto the sofa and reached for her hand. And when he linked his fingers with hers, a jolt of electricity shot up her arm.

"You can't deny our chemistry. I know you can feel it." He brought her hand to his mouth and brushed her knuckles with his lips. And then he teased her with a quick, playful bite.

Gina's blood rushed from her head to her toes. Heat pooled between her legs. Her nipples went hard.

But when he sent her that sly, sexy smile, she jerked her hand back.

Damn him, she thought, as her pulse jumped and jittered. *Damn him to hell.*

He was right, of course. His ploy would work. The tabloids would feed on the sexual frenzy he intended to create. The press would sensationalize her affair with him instead of trashing Baronessa.

But could she actually paw him in public? Or let him run those spine-tingling hands all over her body?

"So, what do you say?" Flint asked. "Are we on?"

Yes. No. Maybe. Her mind spun. Her heart raced. "I don't know. I—"

"Hey, if you're worried about your image, relax. I've got that covered."

She blinked. "What are you talking about?"

He crossed to the bar. "That stiff nature of yours. You know as well as I do that it won't fly, Gina. It'll make you seem unlikable."

She eyed him with annoyance. "Oh, really?"

"Yeah." He popped the top on a soda and took a swig. "But I've dealt with this sort of thing before. I'm just the guy who can give you an image that will dazzle the media, charm the public and make men fall at your feet."

Offended, she lifted her chin. "I don't need you to run my social life."

He set his drink on the table. "The hell you don't. You've got incredible sex appeal, but you don't know how to use it."

"And a phony affair with you is going to turn me into a femme fatale?"

He slanted her his signature grin. "You bet is it."

"Go to hell, Flint."

"Hey, come on. Don't be that way. This is business."

At the moment she didn't care. Refusing to listen to any more of his spin-doctor spiel, she rose and headed for the door, leaving him cursing behind her.

The community living room at the brownstone was cozy yet elegant, with tall, leafy plants, beige furniture and an array of pale blue pillows, but the familiar atmosphere didn't lighten Gina's mood.

Eight hours after her meeting with Flint, she sat on a big, comfy sofa, venting her frustration to her younger sisters.

Rita, an almost twenty-five-year-old nurse at Boston General, listened with a sympathetic ear.

Twenty-three-year-old Maria, on the other hand, seemed preoccupied. She stood beside the window, gazing at the setting sun. Gina admired her sister's business savvy, and tonight she needed the other woman's undivided attention.

"Don't you care about what's going on?" Gina asked, unable to temper her irritation.

Maria turned instantly. She stared at Gina with dark eyes, her chiseled features a mask of composure. In spite of her petite frame, she exuded strength. "That isn't fair. You know how important the Valentine's Day promotion was to me. I'm as concerned as you are about the company our grandparents built."

Of course she was, Gina thought guiltily. Maria managed Baronessa Gelateria, a family-owned, old-fashioned ice-cream parlor—a Hanover Street location overflowing with charm and an emotional cloud of memories.

Still, Gina couldn't help but wonder if there was something else going on in Maria's life. Her sister had been slipping off lately, almost as if she were meeting someone on the sly.

Startled by her imagination, Gina shook her head. The phony affair Flint had proposed had warped her mind. Now she was conjuring a secret lover for Maria.

"I feel like I'm trapped between a rock and a hard place," Gina said, drawing the conversation to her rival. "Baronessa's reputation is floundering, and I just locked horns with the spin doctor who's supposed to pull us out of this mess."

Maria moved away from the window. "I'm sorry, Gina. I know this isn't easy on you."

Rita, seated in one of the overstuffed chairs, tucked her legs beneath her. She still wore her uniform, but she'd removed the white, crepe-soled shoes. "There has to be a solution."

"Yes, but what?" Gina asked. "I'm willing to do whatever it takes to restore Baronessa's reputation, but I can't stand the thought of snuggling up to that macho, arrogant man." She dragged a hand through her hair, tugging her fingers through the loosened, unruly curls. "He doesn't think I can dazzle the media on my own. He thinks I need him to coach me."

"Then prove him wrong," Maria suggested. "Show him that you can handle the press."

Rita perked up. "That's a great idea. After all, Gina, you have your own brand of charm. There's nothing wrong with your image."

"That's right." Maria sent her a warm smile. "You're a beautiful, powerful, successful woman. What can a spin doctor teach you that you don't already know?"

"Nothing," Gina said, her confidence budding. But she could teach Flint Kingman plenty.

After an exhausting ten hours at the office, Flint unlocked his front door, then dropped his keys and spewed a vile curse.

His day had gone from bad to worse, and it was all Gina's fault.

How could she have turned him down? His plan was brilliant. But she was too stubborn to admit it, to thank him the way she should have. He wasn't just offering to repair the damage at Baronessa, he was offering to glamorize her image.

What female in her right mind wouldn't want that?

Didn't she know whom she was dealing with? Flint was an expert. Even his house was a work of art, a renovation with bold lines and stunning curves.

He glanced around, proud of the changes he'd made. His entryway featured hardwood floors instead of cool, marble tiles, and a fluid archway led to a collection of carefully chosen antiques, erotic paintings and a spiral staircase as smooth and sleek as a woman's body. He liked to run his hands along the banister, to feel the architectural beauty it possessed.

After all, he thought, everything, even inanimate objects, represented life.

Suddenly craving a warm shower and a cold beer, he headed to a large, custom-designed kitchen, grabbed a long-neck bottle and started stripping off his clothes.

By the time he climbed the stairs to the master bedroom, he'd left a careless stream of garments strewn along the way.

Standing beside the bed in a pair of pin-striped boxers, he twisted the cap on the beer and took a swig.

And then the damned phone rang.

Still feeling surly about Gina walking out on him, he grabbed the receiver. "What?" he said in place of a proper hello.

"It's me," a feminine voice announced.

"Who's me?" he asked, even though he knew it was the ice princess herself.

"It's Gina. And I changed my mind."

"Did you, now?"

"Yes, I did. After all, it is a woman's prerogative."

"So you'll have that phony affair with me?"

"Yes," she said primly. "But I won't allow you to alter my image."

He glared at the phone for a second. She would take his advice whether she liked it or not. But he wasn't about to argue the point. For now he would let her think she'd won. "Fine, but you can't back out if things get a little rough. So you better be damned sure you're committed to this project."

"I intend to combat the trouble at Baronessa," she retorted. "Even if it means faking a relationship with you."

"All right, then. I'm coming over."

"What for?" she asked suspiciously.

"To work out the details. I'll be there in about an hour."

He hung up before she could protest, then proceeded to peel off his boxers and climb in the shower, hoping to hell she didn't invade his mind. The last thing he needed was to fantasize about Gina Barone again.

To make sure he didn't falter, he turned the water to cold and then cursed when the frigid droplets sprayed him.

Why was he so attracted to her? She was as stiff and corporate-minded as a woman could be. She didn't have a warm, nurturing bone in her body.

And these days Flint wanted someone to care. He wanted a woman who would do anything for him—even give up a thriving career.

It was a selfish thought, but he didn't give a damn. The news about his mother had changed him, and he couldn't help but long for what he'd been denied.

He shut off the icy water and dried vigorously. Then he reached for the abalone shell on his dresser and lit the bundle of sage contained within it. When he was just a boy, his grandmother had taught him to smudge, to purify himself and his surroundings.

Flint walked a somewhat shaky line between the white and Indian worlds, and he supposed he always would. It came with the territory, with being a mixed-blood living in the brain-jarring, fast, furious, ever stimulating pace of the city.

He wanted to raise his future children within the powwow circle, to teach them to dance, but he wondered if that time would ever come. Or if it was meant to be.

With the scent of sage on his skin, he dressed in a pair of black trousers and a gray sweater, preparing to see Gina.

As promised, he arrived at her door within the hour and pressed the intercom to the fourth-floor apartment.

She buzzed him into the building, and he waited for her in the foyer. The brownstone presented a polished-wood staircase, a modern elevator with an old-fashioned gate and a reception area decorated like a living room.

Suddenly Flint could feel a gust of feminine energy swirling around him like a perfumed ghost. He jammed his hands in his pockets, then glanced at the staircase.

Gina descended the steps, looking like a siren from the Italian sea. Her hair fell in a wild mass over her shoulders, each strand rioting in disarray.

Instantly, a surge of sexual heat blasted through his veins.

She reached the foyer, and they stood for a moment, staring at each other.

"I like your hair that way," he said casually, digging his hands deeper into his pockets, where his body had gone hard.

"Thank you," she responded in that cool tone of hers. "But I prefer it up."

Little witch, he thought. She couldn't even take a compliment graciously. He imagined tangling his hands in all those bohemian curls and tugging until she yelped—in pain and in pleasure. "I want you to wear it down when you're with me."

Her chin lifted. "Don't start, Flint."

He flashed a rakish smile, knowing his devil-may-care grin would annoy her. "Don't start what?"

"Telling me what to do."

He shrugged, and she gestured to the reception area. "Have a seat, and I'll pour you a drink."

"Thanks, but I'll have it in your apartment."

She gave him a haughty look. "I'm not inviting you upstairs."

He moved a little closer, crowding her. "Yes, you are. In a few days you and I are going to start dating. That gives me the right to see your place."

She backed away. "Yeah, well, just remember that in a few weeks I'm going to kick you to the curb."

"That's right, you are. And I'm sure you'll enjoy every

minute of it.'' Flint started up the stairs without her. ''But for now you're stuck with me.''

She blew out a windy breath and followed, catching up to him. They reached her apartment at the same time, and she opened the door.

''Nice,'' he said. Very nice. Hardwood floors led to an enticing display of international furnishings. An English writing table sat below a leaded-glass window, and a Chinese vase decorated a stark and stately fireplace mantel. The walls were painted a soft shade of cream and accented with a touch of wine. The sofas, he noticed, were covered in Italian silk.

The lady had taste.

''What would you like to drink?'' she asked.

''Coffee,'' he decided, heading for the kitchen.

He nosed around while she brewed a European blend. ''You can tell a lot about a person by what's in their refrigerator,'' he said. He opened hers and took inventory. She liked to cook, he realized, as he poked through containers of leftovers and a crisper filled with fresh greens.

She leaned against the counter while the coffee brewed. Her kitchen was white, with vintage-style fixtures and a hand-painted porcelain sink. A garden window held a variety of potted herbs, and French doors led to a terrace that overlooked the city.

''What's in your fridge?'' she asked.

''Bachelor stuff.''

She tilted her head. ''Spoiled milk? Pizza growing mold?''

He helped himself to the coffee. ''I'm not that bad.'' Sipping the hot drink, he studied her over the rim of his cup. Her hair was still driving him crazy. She looked as if she'd gone for a quick, hard ride—on a man's lap.

''I want to see your bedroom,'' he said, placing his coffee beside an ornamental decanter.

''No dice, Kingman. My bedroom is off-limits.''

"Not to me. I'm about to become your lover."

"My fake lover," she corrected.

He ignored her and proceeded down the hall, where he assumed her room was. She stalked after him, grumbling about his manners. Or lack of them, he supposed.

He opened her door and stared in shocked silence.

"What's wrong?" she asked from behind him.

"This is my room," he responded, feeling as if she'd invaded his sanctuary. His soul. The emotions driving him.

"What are you talking about?"

He turned to look at her, this woman he barely knew. "I have a cherry armoire that was probably built by the same cabinetmaker. And my bed is almost identical. Even my quilt is the same color." A deep, sensual burgundy, he thought. Like the shade of her lips, the blush on her cheeks.

Gina glanced at the bed, then at him. "Something has to be different."

He walked to her dresser, an eighteenth-century piece similar to the one he'd found in a dusty little antique shop on the West Coast. Somehow they'd chosen nearly the same furniture.

"Did you use a decorator?" he asked.

She shook her head. "No. Did you?"

"No."

They stared at each other from across the room, trapped in an awkward gaze. It almost seemed as if they'd been sleeping in a parallel universe, as if their spirits knew each other from another time or another place.

Searching for a diversion, for an escape from the unwelcome bond, he shifted his attention to the top of her dresser.

And then he noticed the figurines. Some were whimsical and cherubic and others shone like jewels, their wings tipped in gold.

The ice princess collected angels.

Flint looked up and caught a confusing image of Gina.

As she moved toward him, the glow from an amber bulb illuminated her skin and sent highlights dancing through her tousled hair, giving her a heavenly aura.

"They're beautiful, aren't they?" She picked up a gilded figure and held it up to the light, to the halo surrounding her.

For a long, drawn-out moment he couldn't take his eyes off her. He just stood, awed by her beauty, by the sheer radiance of her magic. The tiny statue shimmered gloriously in her hand.

Before he did something stupid, like telling her how exquisite she was, Flint broke the spell.

"I don't believe in angels," he said. It was bad enough she'd stolen his bedroom. He wasn't about to let her con him into thinking she was some sort of celestial being.

A disapproving scowl appeared on Gina's face, and he headed to her walk-in closet and opened the door, determined to get back to work.

She spun, clutching the gold-leafed figurine to her chest. "What are you doing?"

"Checking out your clothes."

"Why? Are you afraid we have the same wardrobe?"

"No, smart aleck. I'm looking for something for you to wear on our first date. Something long and slinky. Maybe a little glittery."

"I don't do slinky."

"You will when you're with me," he told her. One way or another, he intended to turn Gina Barone into a femme fatale. Not an angel, he reminded himself. But a sizzling, sultry she-devil.

A woman who would stir his blood without stirring his heart.

Four

Gina wondered what Flint was up to. He'd gone to her apartment last night, and this afternoon he insisted she come to his office. Supposedly he had a surprise in store.

Although she didn't trust him, she was just curious enough to show up.

When she entered the reception area, Kerry, Flint's loyal assistant, looked up and smiled. The young woman sat at her trendy desk, studying the monitor on her computer.

"He's expecting you," Kerry said. "So you can go right in."

"Thanks." Gina drew a breath and headed down the hall.

She found Flint waiting casually for her arrival with three rolling racks of clothes, shoeboxes stacked a mile high and a full-length, portable mirror at his disposal.

"What's all this?" she asked.

He sent her his spin-doctor smile. "Your wardrobe selection for the next two weeks. I told a stylist what you needed, and she sent them over. She shops for some of the most famous women in the world.''

Gina scanned the racks and took in an eyeful. Evening gowns, bodysuits, skirts that would barely cover her rear.

He reached for a long silver gown. ''Try this one on. You can change in my bathroom. And if it fits, you can wear it tomorrow night.''

She studied the sparkling garment. The neckline plunged in front, in what she assumed would be from her breasts to her navel. ''You've got to be kidding.''

''You'll look hot in this, baby.''

Her full Cs would fall right out of that flimsy contraption. ''If you like it so much, you wear it.''

Not easily deterred, he reached for another gown, a cherry-red, skintight number slit to the hip. ''How about this one? It's got a G-string to match.''

A G-string she was going to use as a slingshot if he foisted one more skimpy dress on her. ''You're not turning me into a bimbo, Flint. So knock it off.''

He jammed the red gown onto the rack. ''You're a prude, Gina.''

She crossed her arms. ''I am not.''

''Oh, yeah?'' He sat on the edge of his desk, his hair falling onto his forehead. ''I'll bet you've never made love on an airplane. Or in an elevator. Or even beneath a big shady tree at the park.''

She tried to act as if his accusation hadn't embarrassed her. Or made her skin warm. ''It's illegal to mess around in public places.''

''True, but that's what makes it so exciting.''

Gina did her damnedest to avoid his gaze, but she could feel those hot amber-flecked eyes shooting sexual sparks right at her.

''I'm a lady,'' she said. ''I behave properly in public.''

''Yeah, but don't you ever want to live out your fantasies?''

"I don't have airplane fantasies."

He cocked his head. "What about elevators?"

Okay, so maybe he had her there, but she wasn't about to admit it. Gina wasn't brave enough to pursue her fantasies, to live on the edge. She drove a luxury sedan instead of a sports car, took practical vacations rather than slip away to unpredictable locations and battled an ulcer that flared up whenever her stress level hit the Richter scale. Which meant sex in an elevator wasn't very likely.

She'd slept with two men her entire life, and both relationships had fallen flat. Her first lover, a striving-for-success executive in a Fortune 500 conglomerate, had been envious of her inheritance, claiming that she didn't work nearly as hard as he did. So she'd gone for a doting, less ambitious partner the next time, but he'd bored her to tears with his hand-patting, milquetoast ways.

"What about in private?" Flint asked.

She glanced up. "I'm sorry? What?"

He reached for a short black dress and gave it a masculine study. Gina thought the leather garment looked like something a dominatrix might wear. She couldn't help but wonder if the stylist had sent over a pair of thigh-high boots, as well.

"Do you behave properly in private?"

Her mouth went dry. She'd never torn off a man's clothes or clawed his back. But she wasn't a Puritan, either. "I behave just fine."

He tossed the minidress at her. "Go put this on. I want to see your legs. All of them, all the way to your thighs."

She caught the leather garment, then felt the smooth texture slide against her skin. "No."

He watched her through those whiskey-flecked eyes. "We're supposed to fool the world into believing we're lovers. You realize that, don't you?"

"Of course, I do. But can't we pretend our first date is

actually our first date instead of posing as lovers right away?''

''Yes, we can do that. But we've only got a few weeks to pull this off, so you're going to have to fall for my charms pretty damn quick.''

Trust Mr. Macho to word it like that. ''Why can't you fall for my charms?''

''Because you'll be dressed like a prude, that's why.''

''Fine, I'll wear something provocative. But I'll shop for myself.'' She hung the whips-and-chains dress on the rack. ''Where are we going, anyway?''

''To the opening of a new play. An erotic play,'' he added. ''So be prepared for a hot, sultry night.''

Gina's heart clamored against her breast. An X-rated production? A hot, sultry night?

''I can handle anything you dish out,'' she told him, even though she was suddenly scared out of her properly behaved wits.

Gina gazed at herself in the mirror. Could she pull this off? Could she actually wear this gown in public?

The seventies style looked like something Tara Shaw would have donned in her heyday. The white fabric clung to Gina's body in a slim, simple line. But that wasn't the problem. The halter dress left her back completely bare. Which meant that she'd forgone a bra—something she'd never done before.

What was wrong with her? Was she trying to compete with a young Tara Shaw? Prove to Flint that she was as daring as his former lover?

Gina checked the clock, and her heart did a somersault. Flint would be here any minute.

She scrambled around the apartment for her shoes and her wrap. And the evening bag containing her stomach medicine.

She nearly tripped putting on her heels, then ran to the mirror for a final inspection.

And that was when she saw one nipple staring at her. Good grief. She looked like a car with a burned out headlight.

Should she arouse the other nipple? Or try to make the erect one recede?

Tilting her head, she frowned. She had no idea how to turn off the shining headlight, so she closed her eyes and rubbed her thumb against the shy breast.

And suddenly an image of Flint invaded her mind—that wild, dream-induced image.

Moonlight bathed him in a hazy glow. Water fell from the sky. The wind blew rain against his face, his arms, his naked chest.

As he moaned his pleasure, she toyed with his fly, working the damp zipper, brushing the hardness—

And then the intercom sounded.

Gina's eyes flew open. She rushed to the door and pressed the button. "Yes?"

Flint's voice came over the speaker. "Are you ready?"

"No. I mean, sort of. Not quite." She needed a moment to breathe, to gain the confidence to face him. Both nipples were painfully aroused. "Wait for me on the first floor, and I'll meet you there."

She buzzed him into the building then raced to the mirror and slipped on a wrap that complemented her dress.

A quick glass of wine would take the edge off, but she feared it would irritate her ulcer. Abandoning the idea, she gave herself a few minutes to calm down.

When she opened the front door, she nearly bumped into Flint.

Cool and collected, he wore a classic black suit, a crisp white shirt and a slim black tie. She detected European cologne and a dash of peppermint, and she assumed he sucked on a breath mint.

She closed the door behind her. "You were supposed to wait for me downstairs."

He flashed a rebellious grin. "Since when do I listen to what you tell me to do? Now take off your jacket and let me see your dress."

"It's a provocative gown," she told him, trying to sound casual. "It'll get me noticed."

"Let me be the judge of that." He reached for the jeweled buttons on her wrap.

"I'll do it." Fidgeting with the sequined jacket, she removed it, did a quick twirl to show him her exposed back and tried to cover up again.

"Hold on. Wait." He snagged the wrap, leaving her vulnerable to his eyes.

Those hot, amber-flecked eyes.

She put her arms at her sides, wishing she hadn't worn a braless-style gown. As he zeroed in on her protruding nipples, she clutched her handbag.

Say something, she thought. *Don't just stand there and stare. Don't remind me that I fantasized about you in front of the mirror.*

He moved closer, and she fought for her next breath. "May I have my jacket back now?"

"No." He draped the sequined wrap over the banister. "I want to look at you some more."

"You're making me nervous, Flint."

"I know."

He moved even closer, and she shuddered.

"Relax. We're supposed to be on the verge of becoming lovers. You can't jump every time I touch you."

He slid his hands into her hair, and she battled a bout of dizziness. "What are you doing?"

"Loosening a few pins." Strands of hair fell, curling around his fingers. "There," he said. "Now you're perfect."

She couldn't imagine how she looked with half her chignon falling down. Tousled, she imagined. As if she'd just tumbled out of bed.

He stepped back and gave Gina her wrap. They took the elevator, and the ride to the first floor seemed to take forever.

"Do you think anyone has ever made love in here?" he asked.

"I doubt it. I mean, no." Her sisters wouldn't do something that like that. Would they? Of course not. Rita and Maria were proper girls, like her.

"We should fake it sometime." A boyish grin tilted his lips. "Pretend we're making out in here."

"That isn't funny." The automatic gate opened, and she bolted out of the elevator, her nipples still protruding like bullets.

Flint and Gina walked to his car. He opened the passenger door and watched her slide into the Corvette.

A moment later, he climbed behind the wheel and latched his seat belt. Gina sat beside him, her hair tumbling around her face. She turned to look at him, and his blood went hot.

Her lips were painted red, just like his car.

The 1963 Sting Ray offered sleek, smooth lines, a split-window design and a fast, fuel-injected ride. The lady, he thought, gave him an even bigger thrill.

He wanted to kiss her, to taste that luscious mouth. But he couldn't, not until they were in a public forum. The seduction was supposed to be for the press.

Flint started the engine, shifted into gear and pulled into traffic. Soon he sped through a yellow light, making it across the intersection before it changed to red. Red meant stop. But tonight, he decided, thinking about Gina's lips, it meant go.

"Have you heard about this play?" he asked.

She nodded. "Yes, but I hadn't planned on seeing it."

"Why not?" He stole a glance at his date and noticed her hands were folded anxiously on her lap. "Because of the nudity?"

"I suppose. I mean, I don't know. I prefer musicals."

He grinned. She was so damn proper. In some ways that turned him on. He liked the idea of corrupting her, even if it was for show. "*Hair* is a musical, and in the production I saw, the cast took off their clothes. Of course, that wasn't exactly erotica." He ran another yellow light and tossed an important detail of their scandal at her. "Speaking of erotica, I arranged for us to pose for a portrait."

Her voice jumped. "What?"

"Kerry's husband is an artist, and he agreed to do this. It'll be great publicity for him. And for us, of course. He'll take some sexy photographs to sketch from. But before he gets a chance to decide which shot to use for the painting, the pictures will be stolen from his studio and sold to the tabloids." Flint kept his eyes on the road. "We'll be the talk of the town."

Gina's breath rushed out. "Sexy photos? You can't mean that."

"It's part of the scandal. A big part of it."

"Why didn't you tell me this before now?"

Because she wouldn't have agreed if she'd known about it in the beginning. "I didn't want to spring everything on you at once."

She crossed her arms. "I'm not doing it. No way am I going to allow you to circulate those kind of pictures of me."

"They'll be pictures of us, not just you."

"I'm not taking off my clothes in front of you or Kerry's husband. So forget it."

"You won't be naked. You'll be wearing lingerie. And Kerry will be there to help you style your hair and touch up your makeup." He pulled into the theater's parking lot. "You don't have a choice, Gina. You've got to do this. It's an important part of the scandal. It will generate all sorts of press.''

''I don't care. I'm still not doing it.''

''The hell you aren't.'' He stopped for valet service, waiting behind other cars. ''You promised you wouldn't back out, even if things got a little rough. And I'm holding you to that promise.''

''You tricked me.''

''I did what I had to do.'' He met her riled gaze. ''This is supposed to be one of those impulsive, whirlwind romances. So it's only natural that I would commission a portrait.''

''Why? Just because Kerry's husband is an artist?''

''No. Because I collect erotic art, and you're my obsession. We're supposed to be falling in love. Even if we're not right for each other.''

She shook her head. ''People don't fall in love in two weeks.''

''People in lust do. Sometimes they don't know the difference.''

Suddenly Gina seemed shy. She glanced down and toyed with her handbag, fingering the jeweled clasp. ''I don't think I can pose like that.''

''Yes, you can. We both can.'' Flint couldn't help himself. He had to touch her.

When he reached out to smooth one of the stray curls from her face, she looked up, and they got caught in a quiet stare.

He brushed her cheek, absorbing the soft, satiny texture of her skin. How could an ice princess feel so warm? So sensual? So sweet and angelic?

''What will be you be wearing?'' she asked.

He withdrew his hand. ''In the pictures?''

She nodded.

''Jeans, no shirt and no underwear, I guess. Kerry's husband said something about me unbuttoning my pants. You know, kind of far down.''

She chewed her bottom lip. "When are we supposed to do the shoot?''

He studied her mouth, her teeth, the way she nibbled her lip. "In two days. So we'll be sleeping together by then. Or pretending to,'' he clarified.

"I guess it could happen tonight. I've never made love on a first date, but this is different. Since we won't really be…doing it.''

"I should probably hang out at your apartment after the play. Just for a few hours, so it seems like we couldn't resist each other. Is that all right with you?''

"Yes,'' she said, as their eyes met again.

A horn honked, and Flint realized he hadn't moved up in line to take his turn. A uniformed valet waved him forward, urging him to pay attention to something other than the beautiful woman with whom he was faking an affair.

The theater was built in Romanesque architecture, with stone columns, a mosaic ceiling and ornamented walls.

The lobby featured plush carpeting and several crowded bars. As Gina and Flint milled through the grand room, her stomach flipped and flopped, and the evening had just begun.

He leaned into her. "Let me help you with your wrap.''

"All right,'' she said, knowing he expected her to remove the only protection she had.

She unbuttoned the sequined jacket, and he stood behind her. His breath stirred against the nape of her neck, making her much too warm. The instant she was free of the wrap, her nipples brushed the clingy fabric of the halter dress.

"You're so beautiful.'' Flint still stood behind her, only now he touched her skin, sliding a finger down her spine, teasing bare flesh.

This was part of the game, she thought. Part of the public

scandal. But his caress was real. And so was her reaction. Every nerve ending in her body came alive, tingling with sensations she hadn't known she possessed.

He put his arms around her and pulled her tight against him. Her rear bumped his fly, and he tugged at her earlobe with his teeth.

Hundreds of people filtered through the lobby, talking and drinking, enjoying the cocktail hour before the show, and all the while Flint had his hands and his mouth all over her. His fingers, she noticed, were dangerously close to her aroused nipples.

"Would you like a drink?" he asked against her ear.

She managed a shaky yes and told him to get her a glass of white wine. Not because she wanted to ply her ulcer with alcohol, but because she needed something to calm her nerves.

"I'll be right back." He headed to the bar, and she smoothed her dress and clutched her jacket, wishing she could cover herself.

In two days she and Flint would pose for pictures. Erotic photographs.

Dear God. What had she gotten herself into?

"Gina?" A familiar, feminine voice spoke her name. "Is that you?"

She glanced up and saw Morgan Chancellor, the business associate who'd given her the scoop on Flint and Tara Shaw. "Hello, Morgan. Of course, it's me."

"Oh, my. You look simply ravishing."

"Thank you. I'm on a date."

"Yes, I saw your escort. You're with Flint." Morgan glanced in the direction of the closest bar. "I guess you two are hitting it off."

Gina fidgeted with her wrap. "He's an intriguing man."

"Yes, he is." The socialite lowered her voice to a discreet whisper. "And I can tell you've been kissing him.

Darling, you need to fix your lipstick. It's terribly obvious."

"Is it?" Struggling to play her part, Gina reached into her purse and removed a compact. She hadn't been kissing Flint. She'd been fretting about those upcoming photos, chewing anxiously on her lips, then licking the lipstick from her teeth.

She reapplied the racy red color and smiled at Morgan. "I couldn't help myself."

"I don't blame you a bit. But be careful. He'll take you for a walk on the wild side."

"That's the idea. To be quite honest, I'm tired of being a good girl. And I need a diversion, something to help me forget about the trouble at Baronessa."

"Then you found the right guy. And he chose the perfect event. I've heard this production is absolutely decadent. Which is why I couldn't stay away. Of course, I'm here with some girlfriends. My husband isn't comfortable around this sort of thing."

Neither am I, Gina thought.

Flint returned with her wine. He greeted Morgan and slid his arms around Gina's waist.

"I should get back to my friends," the redhead said. "You two enjoy your evening."

Flint smiled. "Thanks. We will."

As Morgan walked away, he nuzzled Gina's neck. "Did you miss me?" he whispered.

She took a gulp of wine, then turned in his arms. "Maybe we should find our seats." Her knees had gone weak, and she needed to sit.

"Okay, baby."

He stroked her cheek, brushing it tenderly with the back of his hand, and for a moment, she almost wished the affection was real.

Flint Kingman was a damn fine actor. But his mother had been a Hollywood starlet, so acting was in his blood.

As they located their seats, Gina wondered if she should tell him she'd purchased a movie his mother had costarred in. She'd watched the film three times, awed by the young woman's beauty. Flint had inherited his mother's stunning cheekbones, her natural sex appeal, her sly, flirtatious smile. He was, without a doubt, Danielle Wolf's son.

And then, of course, there was his scandalous affair with Tara Shaw. She imagined that had shaped Flint into who and what he was, as well.

Gina turned to look at him, and suddenly a strange thought hit her. Had he truly made love to Tara? Or had their relationship been a publicity stunt? Something to boost the aging actress's career?

"What are you thinking about?" he asked.

"Nothing," she said. Nothing but his ex-lover. Or his fake ex-lover. With Flint, anything could be a lie.

Within thirty minutes, the theater was full. As the lights dimmed and the curtain opened, Gina stared at the stage.

The opening scene stunned the audience. A young woman began to undress in front of a mirror. When she was completely naked, she closed her eyes and touched her nipples, slowly, seductively, whispering a man's name.

Gina nearly gasped. She'd done the same thing this evening. She'd stood in front of a mirror, thinking about Flint.

Smoke filled the stage, and a man appeared. It was a dream sequence, Gina realized. But that didn't stop the dream man from taking the flesh-and-blood woman into his arms.

And teasing her with foreplay.

Gina knew they were only acting. But their performances affected her nonetheless.

Heat pooled between her legs. An erotic chill raced up her spine. She felt what the actress was feeling—fire, moisture, a prelude to sex.

And when Flint moved closer, she knew the scene aroused him, too.

Suddenly the stage went dark. There was no light, only the sighs of lovemaking, the whispers of a dream.

In the blackness, Flint ran his hand along the side of Gina's dress, pressing against her rib cage, the fullness of her breast, her bare arm.

She turned her head, and he kissed her.

Hard.

So hard, her breath rushed into his.

The woman on stage was climaxing, making throaty little sounds. Lights flickered on and off, flashing naked images of the actors, but Flint kept kissing Gina.

As he delved into her hair, he wrapped his hands around the curls that fell and tugged her closer.

His tongue took hers over and over. He was hot and demanding, rough and insistent. He made her want; he made her ache. Yet somehow, he made her part of him.

Overwhelmed with pleasure, she kissed him back, uncovering a flavor so rich and forbidden, she hungered for more.

In the next instant, light flooded the stage, and the woman was alone.

Gina pulled away and stared at Flint. She could see the shadowy outline of his face, and she knew he was her dream man. Her fantasy. The actor who would disappear when their scandal ended.

Heaven help her, she thought. She was trapped in a torrid affair that wasn't even real.

Five

Flint stood in front of Gina's living room window, staring out at Boston's North End. They'd just returned from the theater, and he couldn't get his emotions in check.

"What should we do now?" she asked.

Kiss, he thought. *Touch. Make love.* Suddenly he wanted the affair to be real. He wanted to sleep with Gina, to have a wild, passionate, fire-induced fling with the ice princess and get her out of his system.

"Nothing," he said. "We don't have to do anything."

"Should I make some tea? It's late, so maybe we should have a herbal brew. How about chamomile? I have home-made muffins, too."

He turned to look at her. She still wore the backless white dress, and her hair still tumbled from its confinement. They'd kissed over and over during the play and during the brightly lit intermission, creating a public scene. And now she was suggesting a spot of chamomile and a plate of leftover muffins. Hell, it might as well be tea and crumpets with the queen.

"We're supposed to be bumping and grinding, Gina. Screwing each other's brains out."

Her face flushed. "Don't think you'll be taking your sexual frustration out on me."

He held her gaze. He knew her mouth tasted as luscious as it appeared, and somehow that only made him angrier. "Why not? You caused it."

"And you're a crude, unfeeling man."

Unfeeling? He ached for her. He hurt so badly, he could barely breathe. "I have plenty of feelings." *Too many,* he thought.

"This isn't easy on me, either." She tried to smooth her hair and gave up when she encountered a handful of disheveled curls. "I'm attracted to you, Flint. But I'm not going to sleep with you. I'm not going turn this into a real affair."

Defensive, he jammed his hands in his pockets. "Did I say that's what I wanted?"

"No, but I thought some tea would take the edge off. You know, to keep our minds from straying in that direction." She dropped her gaze to the floor. "Maybe you should just go home."

Damn her. Why did she have to look so vulnerable? "I'm sorry. I didn't mean to offend you. It's just been a weird night." First the show at the theater, and now he was in her apartment trying to establish a cover in case anyone in the neighborhood was watching. "If I leave now, it won't seem as if we made love. I've only been here for ten minutes."

She didn't respond. She seemed shy, her gaze riveted to the floor.

Unsure what to do, he shifted his stance. Part of him wanted to go home and never see her again, while another part imagined carrying her to bed.

"So, is it all right if I stay for a while?" he asked, his voice a bit too rough.

She glanced up, and they stared at each other. The energy between them remained thick, and so did the air in his lungs.

Finally she nodded, and Flint forced a breath. He hadn't expected this to happen, at least not to this degree. He was so damn sure he could handle his attraction to her. But here he was, stuck in a state of arousal.

"Maybe you should brew that tea," he said.

"Will you drink some?"

"Sure." He didn't particularly care for tea, but he knew she needed to refine the rest of their evening, to make it seem proper somehow.

She turned away, and he sat on the couch and stared at the blank TV screen.

When she returned, he noticed she'd laced the tray with heated muffins, sugar, cream, lemon wedges and honey. He wondered what she would do if he revealed that he had a honey fetish. That one of his fantasies was drizzling the sticky substance all over a woman's body and licking her until she—

"Do you want a muffin?" Gina gestured to a flowered plate. "These are blueberry and those are bran."

Guilty, Flint froze. "No, thanks." He kept his eyes away from the honey, especially when she spread some onto a muffin and nibbled daintily.

If she moaned, he was going to lose it. He would jump right out of his skin.

She sat next to him, picked up the remote control and turned on the TV. He tasted the unappealing tea and studied the flickering images.

She changed the channel repeatedly, the way he did at home when he was bored. But he knew Gina wasn't bored. She was nervous.

"Maybe we should watch a movie," she said. "I have a fairly large selection."

She rifled through her videos and DVDs, and he figured she would offer a girly movie, a chick flick that would calm her down. He would rather get absorbed in guts and glory, in a good, old-fashioned war picture, but he decided to be polite and keep his mouth shut, something he rarely did around her.

"How about this?" She held up *The Caine Mutiny,* and he stared at her in stunned silence. That was one of his all-time favorite films, a Humphrey Bogart vehicle about a crazed captain and his crew.

"What's the matter?" she asked.

"Nothing. I like that movie."

"Me, too. I had a pug named Captain Queeg, but he died a few years ago."

Again, Flint could only stare. "That's not my dog's name, but that's what I call him when he goes nuts and digs up the yard." Flint owned a Jack Russell terrier that kept his gardeners cursing into their shovels.

"Oh, my God. That's so strange. My Captain Queeg wasn't crazy, but he loved strawberries."

"Really?" They looked at each other and laughed. The strawberry scene in *The Caine Mutiny* was a classic.

Without another word, they settled into the evening and watched an old movie, even though they were trying to fool the world into believing they were making long, hard, passionate love.

What had she gotten herself into? Gina sat in front of a lighted mirror, taking deep, anxious breaths.

Kerry stood behind her, putting the final touches on her hair. Flint's assistant had decided that Gina should wear her hair loose for the photo shoot. But that wasn't the problem.

The wardrobe selection troubled her. A red silk nightgown clung to her curves, outlining her breasts and show-casing a pair of skimpy lace panties.

"You're ready," Kerry said.

Gina gazed at the other woman in the mirror, catching both their reflections. She wanted to back out, to say she couldn't go through with this, but she put on a brave front instead.

She came to her feet and accepted the matching robe Kerry offered. She belted it with shaky fingers, and they left the tiny makeup room and entered the studio.

The first thing Gina noticed was the prop that had been brought in for the shoot—a king-size bed, draped in red and white satin.

She scanned the rest of the room and zeroed in on Flint. He leaned against a small table, chatting with Lewis, Kerry's slightly eccentric husband.

Flint glanced over and spotted her. When their eyes met, her heart leaped to her throat. He wore a pair of faded Levi's and little else. His feet and chest were bare. His stomach corded in a six-pack of hard-earned muscle.

Lewis turned, as well. "I see our lady has arrived on the set." He came toward her, but Flint remained where he was.

"Would you like a glass of wine?" Lewis asked. "It'll help you relax."

"Thanks, but I'm okay."

He tilted his head, looking like the artist he was. He wore his bleached hair short and spiked, and both ears possessed multiple piercings. "Are you sure? This is a pretty heavy shoot."

"I can handle it," she lied. "I don't need a drink." She wanted to down an entire bottle of wine, but her ulcer had been acting up for the past few days, and alcohol would only irritate her condition.

"Then let's get started." Lewis instructed Gina and Flint to stand at the foot of the bed while he fiddled with his camera. Kerry adjusted the lights, leaving Flint and Gina to their own devices.

Was Flint nervous, too? She'd never seen him so quiet.

"This is strange, isn't it?" she said, struggling to make conversation.

He nodded. "Yeah, it is."

They both lapsed into silence. Gina glanced at the bed and noticed the lace-edged pillows. The stage was beautifully set, with two tall, wrought-iron candelabras on either side of the bed. Burning candles filled the room with scented wax, giving it a romantic ambience.

"Okay," Lewis called from behind the camera lens. "It's show time."

Flint took a step toward Gina, then skimmed her cheek, brushing her skin with the back of his hand. She liked the sweet, butterfly sensation, but the photographer wasn't impressed.

"Come on, Flint," he coaxed. "You can do better than that. You collect erotic art. You know what this is all about."

Gina lowered her gaze and stared at Flint's naked chest. She knew he collected erotic art, but somehow she hadn't let herself think too deeply about it. Now that seemed impossible.

He reached for the belt on her robe, and she gulped the air in her lungs. What kind of erotic art did he favor? Slim, sultry women in provocative poses? Or hot, hungry couples engaged in illicit acts?

He pushed the robe from her shoulders, and the garment fell to the floor. She stood before him, dressed in the clingy red nightgown, her nipples brushing the fire-tinged silk.

Somewhere in the back of her whirling mind, she heard a clicking sound. Lewis must be taking pictures, capturing the moment.

Flint leaned in close and kissed her, and she ignored the camera. His mouth proved warm and wet, gentle yet demanding. He tasted of breath mints and beer, of masculine beauty and spring lust.

"Take off his belt," she heard Lewis say.

Yes, Gina thought. She wanted to touch Flint, and she hardly cared that Lewis and Kerry watched.

She reached for Flint's belt and felt a shiver rack his body. They stopped kissing and stared at each other. She unhooked the silver buckle. The metal was cold, but his skin, that bronzed flesh, radiated heat.

She pulled the leather through his pant loops, and Lewis instructed her to toss the belt onto the bed and undo Flint's jeans.

Okay, she told herself. She could do this. But after releasing the first two buttons, she bumped a slight hardness beneath Flint's fly, and her fingers froze. He was partially aroused, turned on by her touch.

"Keep going," Lewis prodded.

She bit her lip and went after the third button.

"Good," the artist crooned. "Now drop to your knees."

Stunned, Gina gazed at Flint. He sent her a boyish smile, and her heartbeat skittered.

This wasn't real, she reminded herself. This photo session was as phony as their affair.

Sliding down his body, she landed on her knees and looked at him. She noticed a line of hair that started just below his navel and disappeared into the open waistband of his jeans.

Gina wanted to trace it with her nail, but she didn't dare. Flint couldn't take his eyes off her, and she could barely breathe. This position left her dizzy.

"That's perfect," Lewis said, pleased by what he assumed was their professionalism. "Okay, now, Flint, twist your hands in her hair. Yeah, just like that. And, Gina, play with his jeans. Tug at them a little."

She did as she was told, and after the shoot ended, she came to her feet and teetered on a pair of stiletto heels.

No one spoke, not even Lewis. He gathered his equipment, and Kerry reached for Gina's robe and handed it to her.

The fading sun shone through the skylight, sending streams of gold across a stark white floor. Although the satin-draped bed remained unused, Flint's belt lay across it, reminding Gina of what they'd done.

He turned away to fasten his jeans, and when he spun around, she glanced at his fly and felt her skin warm. She'd seen just enough to trigger her imagination.

He cleared his throat, and she tightened her robe, wondering how they were going to face each other over the casual, late-day lunch they'd agreed upon earlier.

Flint stared at the road. Gina sat beside him, looking prim and proper, but he couldn't get the other image of her off his mind.

The one of her on her knees. That tousled hair, those violet-colored eyes, the slim, silky nightgown displaying every curve.

He would never be the same.

Flint shifted in his seat. He was still aroused, still battling the body part that refused to behave.

"I'm not really in the mood to deal with the public," he said. "So maybe we should skip the diner."

"Do you want to get take-out?" she asked.

Did he? Going to her house didn't seem like a good idea. And he wasn't about to bring her to his place, not when all he could think about was getting her on her knees.

"Why don't we just eat in the car?" He motioned to a hamburger stand across the street. "Is that all right with you?"

She nodded. "Sure. I could go for a milk shake."

"Yeah. Me, too." Something cold, he thought. Something to douse the fire burning inside him.

He headed for the drive-up menu, and they ordered the

same meal. They did that fairly often, he noticed. They liked the same kind of food, the same movies, the same type of furniture.

He parked in a shady spot, and they divided their lunch. When she ate a French fry and licked the salt from her fingers, he nearly groaned.

Was she still wearing those wispy red panties she'd had on under the nightgown? Flint still wore the same jeans, the old, threadbare Levi's she'd had her hands all over.

She glanced at him, and their eyes met. In the next instant they stared at each other in silence. He unwrapped his burger, but the sound of paper rattling made their discomfort even more obvious.

Damn it. Say something. Break the tension.

"It was weird, wasn't it?" he asked.

"The photo shoot?" She toyed with a French fry. "Yes, it was."

"But you did well, Gina." Really well, he thought, recalling the feel of her fingers against his fly.

She dropped her gaze, and he realized how truly shy she was. The ice princess never failed to confuse him.

"Thank you. You did well, too, Flint."

He took a bite of his burger. "Thanks."

"When will the pictures hit the tabloids?" she asked.

"If everything goes according to schedule, they'll be in the next issue."

"That soon?"

"Yep. That soon." He squirted ketchup onto a napkin. "And the media attention we've been getting is nothing compared to the frenzy those pictures are going to generate."

"So we better value our privacy while we've got the chance?"

"Exactly."

She dipped into the ketchup, and their gazes locked again. He wanted to kiss her, but he knew better. Their affair had been created for public display, not for quiet, breathless moments.

She finally ate the fry, leaving him fixated on her mouth.

"Do you have an extra set of keys to the brownstone?" he asked.

She blinked. "Yes. Why?"

"Because I need a set."

She blinked again. "Why?"

"So I don't have to wait for you to let me in. Once the media frenzy starts, the reporters are going to follow us. I don't want to be stuck on your stoop with cameras flashing in my face."

"I've never given a man keys to my house before."

"I'll give them back once this is over." He took another bite of his burger, then paused to swallow his food. "I've never given anyone keys to my place, either."

Gina tilted her head. "Not even Tara Shaw?"

Flint didn't want to talk about the past. "That was ages ago. And I was staying in Hollywood at the time."

"Which means what?" She righted her posture. "I can't figure you and Tara out. I'm not even sure that your affair with her was real."

Suddenly irritated, he tapped his fingers on the steering wheel. "My relationship with Tara is none of your business."

"Why? Because you were faking it? Just like you're faking it with me? You're probably not capable of a real relationship."

Flint snarled. As usual, the ice princess had tossed his attitude in his face. "Me?" he retorted. "What about you? You probably fake orgasms."

"I do not, you big jerk."

Then prove it, he wanted to say. *Climb onto my lap and—*

"I can't wait until this phony affair is over." She moved

closer to the window, as far away from him as she could get.

"You and me both." But that didn't stop him from wanting her. "Hurry up and finish your food. I'm taking you home." He didn't need the aggravation of being near her, of fighting the pressure in his loins.

"Fine. I'm done." She jammed her half-eaten meal into the bag.

He followed suit and peeled out of the parking lot, barely giving her time to latch her seat belt. Speeding through traffic, he cursed to himself.

Women were nothing but trouble.

"You drive like an idiot," she complained.

"So sue me." He had a fast car and raging hormones. That gave him the right to be an idiot.

He turned onto Paul Revere Way and shoehorned his way into a parking spot. They both exited the Vette at the same time.

She gave him a haughty look. "What are you doing?"

"Walking you to your door."

"Don't bother. I can manage just fine without you."

"Too bad." He strolled beside her. The brownstone was at the other end of the street, and he was determined to get her there. And, he supposed, to annoy her on the way.

He reached for her hand, and when she tried to pull away, he held it tighter. "We're on a public street, Gina. So be a good girl and play your part."

She bit her nails into his skin.

"Are you one of those women who claws a man's back, too?" he asked, giving her a smug smile.

"Wouldn't you like to know?" She tossed her head and dug her nails deeper into his hand.

At this point he would take what he could get. Pain, pleasure. He didn't give a damn, as long as it gave him a forbidden thrill.

When they reached the brownstone, he grabbed her and pushed her against the door.

"Don't you dare—"

He cut her off with a kiss. A brutal, desperate, open-mouthed kiss.

She didn't fight him. She took his tongue with the same fury, the same passion, the same angry heat that welled inside him.

He rubbed against her, showing her how hard he was. She slid her hands around his waist and pulled him even closer.

They practically ate each other alive, sucking and licking and hissing like a couple of alley cats.

And then she shoved him away.

"I hate you," she said.

"I hate you, too." He shot the words back, aching to make love to her.

Without another word, he turned and walked away. Did he hate Gina, or hate what she did to him? Somehow, they seemed like the same thing.

Six

Three days later, Gina sat in the community living room at the brownstone, waiting for Flint to arrive.

Another date.

She didn't know how much more of this she could take. They'd avoided each other since their last heated encounter, but he'd finally called and insisted it was time for another public appearance. So here she was, attired in a short, body-hugging dress and a pair of spiky-heeled pumps that added three inches to her already towering height.

She'd purchased the outfit to get back at Flint. She knew the show of legs would drive him crazy. And the push-up bra she'd chosen shoved her breasts up and almost out of her dress, giving her an extra boost of cleavage. Flint would be lusting after what he couldn't have.

And that served the jerk right.

She checked her watch. Where was he, anyway? Of all nights to keep her waiting. She was already on edge, the anger inside her building to a raging inferno.

Why was he so damn secretive about Tara Shaw? Why wouldn't he admit if their relationship had been real or not?

Gina stood and pushed back her hair. She'd whipped her curly mane into a long, tousled mass, scrunching it with a mega-hold hair spray.

Tara Shaw had nothing on her.

Footsteps sounded on the stairs, and she turned to see Rita descending.

"Wow." Her sister stopped to stare. "What a transformation. You're as slinky as a black cat on Halloween."

And just as dangerous, Gina hoped. "Thanks. I intend to make him suffer."

"So I see."

Rita moved forward. And then she flashed a coy, feminine smile. She had a caring, loving nature, but her smile was often laced with mischief. Gina supposed it came with the territory. Rita was a serious woman, dedicated to her career, but the nurse, like many others in her profession, possessed a wry, sometimes playful sense of humor.

Rita went into the kitchen and started a pot of tea. Gina followed her, her high heels clicking on the tiled floor.

"Are you any closer to figuring out who your secret admirer is?" Gina asked.

Rita shook her head and sighed. "No."

On Valentine's Day, her sister had received a small white box tied with a gold ribbon. Inside, she'd found a pin—a small pewter heart with a gold-toned Band-Aid wrapped around it. The gift had been left at the hospital, which led her to believe her secret admirer was affiliated with Boston General.

"I wear the pin on my uniform every day," Rita said. "I keep hoping whoever gave it to me will notice and come forward and identify himself."

He could be an orderly, Gina thought. Or a male nurse. Or maybe even a patient who'd been released by now. "You may never find out."

"I can't imagine someone giving me a gift, then just disappearing."

"Men are hard to fathom," Gina said, thinking about Flint. And they were darn good at keeping secrets. Flint hadn't revealed a thing about himself, particularly his mysterious so-called fling with that Hollywood bombshell.

Maybe he really did have an affair with Tara. Or maybe he'd been in love with her.

Then again, he didn't seem capable of deep emotion.

After a cup of tea, Rita went to her apartment, leaving Gina waiting for Flint.

Where was he?

Finally, the buzzer sounded, announcing his late arrival. She let him into the building and gauged his reaction while he simply stared at her.

For the longest time he didn't speak, but his Adam's apple bobbed with each rough, masculine swallow.

Was he having trouble breathing?

Gina sent him an innocent smile. "Is something wrong?"

"What? No. Everything's just fine. I'm just peachy keen." He loosened the tie around his neck.

"You don't look fine." He looked flushed. And aroused. And gorgeous as ever. He wore an impeccably tailored suit and a shirt that matched the gold flecks in his eyes.

Her dress was gold, too, with just a hint of shimmer. For once she refused to let him intimidate her. He deserved to drool over her. This evening she would tease him into a sexual frenzy, then punish him by making him sleep alone.

He held out his hand.

Confused, she gazed at his palm.

"Give me the keys," he said. "I told you on the phone to have them ready."

"Oh, of course. It nearly slipped my mind." She opened her purse and removed an extra set of keys to the brownstone.

He snatched them and jammed them into his pocket. And then he stared at her again, like a man craving the forbidden. A muscle ticked in his jaw, and his chest heaved with a laden breath.

No doubt, he wanted to shove her against the wall and take what he wanted. But he wouldn't, of course. Stealing a kiss wasn't the same as stealing a woman's entire body.

Revenge was sweet, she thought, feeling like the femme fatale he'd claimed he could turn her into. Only she'd done it without his help. "We're going dancing, right?"

"That's right. To a hot spot downtown."

"That's perfect. Because I'm in the mood to party." She intended to get downright tipsy. How else could she parade around in public with her dress hiked to her rear and her breasts pushed up to her chin? Staying sober was out of the question.

"Let's go," she said, grabbing her jacket. Tonight she wasn't in the mood to worry about what the alcohol would do to her ulcer.

Tonight she would throw caution to the wind and drive Flint Kingman half mad.

Gina was driving him crazy. The hair, the dress, the cleavage he couldn't stop staring at. And if one more guy approached her to dance, Flint was going to kick some serious ass.

Nobody, but nobody put moves on his woman.

Okay, so maybe she didn't exactly belong to him. But they'd been linked together in the society pages, and the tabloids had already picked up on their affair, even though those sexy pictures hadn't surfaced yet.

As far as the world knew, Gina Barone was his.

She sat across from him at the trendy club, sucking on a maraschino cherry.

"I think I'd like to try a pink lady next," she said.

He watched her mouth form a pretty little O around the

cherry. He'd like to try a pink lady, too. But not the kind she referred to.

She'd been sipping one fruity concoction after the other, crunching ice cubes and toying with swizzle sticks and tiny umbrellas. She'd started off with a Midori sour, switched to a blue Hawaii, then went for a tequila sunrise.

"You're not supposed to mix drinks, Gina."

"I'm experimenting tonight."

Yeah, with his hormones. "You're half drunk already."

She tossed her head and sent that wild hair flying. "We're supposed to be out on the town, causing a scene, aren't we?"

I created a monster, he thought. *A tall, slim, high-heeled monster.* "Maybe you should eat something." He pushed a plate toward her.

She dropped the cherry in her glass and picked up a potato skin. After she tasted it, she made a surprised face. "It's spicy."

He shifted in his seat and watched her eat. The potato skins were flavored with cheddar cheese, sour cream and jalapeño peppers. Apparently she hadn't realized he'd ordered an array of spicy appetizers.

She swallowed the bite in her mouth, took a drink and then came to her feet.

"What are you doing?" he asked.

"I'm going to show you how hot it was."

Within a heartbeat, she stood in front of him, wedged herself between his legs and flung her arms around his neck. They were face to face but not quite mouth to luscious mouth.

The air in his lungs shot out. His blood sizzled. The muscles in his stomach flexed in anticipation.

She ran her tongue over her lips, sending his entire body into overdrive.

"Are you going to kiss me or not?" he asked, cursing his weakness, his desperate, all-consuming need for her.

She brushed his mouth in a gentle tease. He suspected half the people in the club were watching. And that aroused him even more. He wanted everyone to know the ice princess was his lady.

His pink lady.

"First you have to tell me your deepest, darkest fantasy," she said.

He caught his breath. Would she be this naughty in bed? "I have a honey fetish."

"Oh, my." She lowered her chin and gave him a sultry stare. "What else?"

He ran his hands along her waist, then down her hips, mesmerized by each rounded curve. "Women in short skirts." He raised her dress just a little. "With no panties."

"Do you want me to take my panties off for you, Flint?"

Yes. Oh, yes. He did. "Right now? Right here?"

She laughed and nipped his ear. "Only if you unzip your trousers for me."

This was insane. This incredible, heart-stopping, thrill-seeking attraction. They were good together. So damn good.

She finally kissed him, putting her mouth over his and sucking his tongue with a vengeance. He sucked back, over and over again. She tasted like tequila, rum and melon liqueur.

And peppers. He could taste the jalapeños.

She pulled back. "Hot, isn't it?"

Like a fever, he thought. "Will you get on your knees for me again, Gina?"

She raised her eyebrows. "Here? Now?"

No. When they were alone. When the public wasn't watching. When he could have her all to himself.

Struck by a jolt of fear, Flint gazed into Gina's eyes.

Heaven help him, he wanted her all to himself. But not just for mindless sex. Suddenly he craved something deeper, something substantial, something to fill the ache.

And that scared the hell out of him.

She wasn't just stirring his libido; she was tapping into his need for emotional security.

"So, do you want me on my knees?" she asked.

"Why not?" He tried to sound casual, to keep his voice even, his breathing steady. "I'll bet it would make the papers."

She tossed a flirtatious smile at him. "I think we'd get arrested instead."

"Yeah, but being hauled off to jail would get us some extra publicity." He hugged her a little closer, not quite able to let go.

"This is fun," she said.

"What? Messing around in public?"

"No. Torturing you."

The ache came back. Tenfold. Damn her, anyway.

He should have known. The little witch only wanted to make him suffer. She'd turned their attraction into a heartless game. Maybe she really did have ice flowing through her veins.

She wrestled out of his arms. "I think I'm ready for that pink lady now."

Fine. He'd let her get drunk. What the hell did he care? This phony affair would be over soon. And then he could find another woman to replace her. Someone sincere. Someone kind. Someone to get Gina Barone out of his system.

On Thursday afternoon, the telephone jangled in Gina's ear. She moaned and reached for the receiver.

"Hello?"

"Why aren't you at work today?"

She recognized Flint's hard-edged voice. "Because I'm sick."

"You've been sick for days. You're blowing our scandal. Get out of bed and get yourself together. I'm taking you out.''

"Leave me alone.'' She drew her knees to her chest. Her stomach burned like a furnace.

"No one has a hangover for that long.''

"I do.''

"Bull. You're just too chicken to face the press.''

"I am not.'' She squinted at the tabloids on her nightstand. At her request, her secretary had brought them by. Those racy pictures had come out yesterday, and they were causing quite a stir. Her reputation would never be the same. "I just need some recovery time. I told you. I'm sick.''

"And I told you to get your butt out of bed.''

Gina glared at the phone. Flint had been calling her every day, making her illness worse. His constant badgering only heightened the stress.

She had enough to worry about. When those photos had hit the newsstand, she'd heard from everyone in her family, everyone but her dad. Of course, her mother had relayed a message. Her father wasn't pleased. He thought she'd gone too far.

Never mind that she'd done it for Baronessa Gelati. That she'd sacrificed her personal reputation to save the company. Her dad never awarded her with professional credit. He never treated her like a business equal.

"Are you still there?'' Flint asked.

"Yes.''

"Then get up and get ready. We need to be seen, Gina. To make a public appearance.''

"Back off, Flint.''

"Damn it, woman.''

She snarled at the receiver again. "I'm hanging up on you.''

"You better not—''

Making good on her threat, she pushed the Talk button

and cut him off. And when the phone rang again, she refused to answer it.

Exhausted, she rolled over and went back to sleep.

An hour later she awakened in a stupor. Peering through hazy vision, she squinted.

Flint stood over her bed like the grim reaper. He wore a long black raincoat, and his features hardened around a snarl. His cheekbones were as sharp as knives, his hair ravaged by the wind.

Dear God. A nightmare. She closed her eyes again until his voice jumped out at her.

"You look like hell, Gina."

She sat up and grabbed her pillow. He was real. Much too real. "What are you doing here?"

"I have a key, remember?"

"That doesn't give you the right to invade my privacy."

"I have the right to check up on you. To make sure you're all right."

Trust a spin doctor to act as if he cared, to put a spin on his actions. "That's all fine and dandy, but I can't deal with you right now."

He sat on the edge of the bed and gave her a level stare. She pushed the covers away, wishing she had the strength to push him away. Why couldn't he let her suffer in peace?

He raised an eyebrow at her. "Charming outfit. It's so slinky. So seductive. So perfect for your new image."

She glanced at her baggy sweats. "I told you, I'm sick."

"What exactly is the nature of your illness? And don't toss that hangover crap at me. You can hold your liquor better than that."

Wanna bet? she thought. "I have a stomachache."

He made a face. "Why? Is it your moon time?"

Her moon—? Good grief. "Are you asking about my period?"

He made another face. "Women get cramps, don't they? And PMS and all that."

She rolled her eyes. "If I told you that was my problem, would you go away?"

"No. But a more conventional man would, I suppose. So, is that your problem?"

Hell's bells. She knew he wouldn't let the subject go until she admitted why she'd been holed up in bed for half the week.

"I have an ulcer, Flint. But keep your mouth shut about it. I don't want my family to know."

His eyebrows furrowed. "Is it bleeding?"

"No. I'm just suffering from the aftereffects of all that alcohol. And the spicy food." Jalapeño potato skins, Cajun chicken wings, curry-seasoned rice balls.

He removed his coat and tossed it over the back of a chair. "How long have you had this condition?"

"For years. But it tends to heal and then recur when I'm under stress. Or when I eat or drink something that doesn't agree with me."

Flint shook his head. "Where does it hurt?"

"Here." She placed her hand under her breastbone.

"I wish you would have told me earlier. I never would have let you eat all that stuff. Or get drunk."

"I don't need a nursemaid."

"The hell you don't." He stood and blew a frustrated breath. "I'm going to get you some milk. That helps, doesn't it?"

"Yes." She almost smiled. The big, gorgeous oaf was acting as if this was his fault. Of course, in a way, it was. He was a major stress factor.

"Should I warm it?"

"Sure." That sounded cozy. And deep down, she liked the idea of Flint waiting on her.

"I'll be right back."

She curled up again, and he returned with a coffee mug filled with warm milk. She accepted the drink and sipped gratefully.

He scooted into bed next to her. "Have you seen a doctor?"

"Yes, and I already took my medicine."

They sat in silence for a while. Her stomach still hurt, but the milk managed to coat the burn. Finally she finished the last of the soothing liquid and handed him the empty cup.

He put it on her nightstand. "You can go back to sleep if you want."

"That's okay. Maybe later." She turned to study his windblown appearance, his tousled hair and rumpled shirt. "Why do you look so beat?"

"I had to fight my way into the building. The vultures are hanging out at your front door."

She tried not to groan. "The press?"

"Yep." He smoothed a curl from her cheek. "We should probably spend our free time at my house in the future. All that ruckus isn't fair to your sisters."

"Will going to your house really make a difference?"

"Sure. If the reporters follow us to my place after a date, they won't be hanging out here."

"That makes sense." She grimaced. "So, what do you think of our photo debut?"

He reached for one of the tabloids. "I think we look pretty damn sexy."

To say the least. The picture on the cover portrayed them as they'd felt that day. Consumed with lust. Gina was on her knees, tugging at his pants. His fly was partially open, revealing rock-hard abs, a masculine navel and a slight shadow of hair that led to a part of him that wasn't visible but was still apparent through his jeans.

Gina leaned forward to assess her printed image. The red nightgown revealed the outline of her breasts and the blatant peaks of her nipples. Desire, she noticed, still studying the photo, burst onto the page, like a ravenous, powerfully winged raptor.

"If they could see us now," she said, nudging his arm.

"Yeah." He grinned, and they both laughed.

When their laughter faded, he said, "We're going to have to carry on this affair a bit longer than we'd originally planned. But I'm not pushing you. Take as much time as you need to feel better."

"Promise not to tell my family?"

"They must know you're sick. And besides, isn't your sister a nurse?"

"My family thinks I have the flu." Whenever her ulcer flared to this degree, she did her best to fool everyone, particularly Rita. It wasn't easy, but she'd gotten away with it so far. "Promise me, Flint."

He frowned at her.

"Please," she implored.

"Okay. I promise."

"Thank you." She closed her eyes and snuggled against him. He felt big and strong. And for now she needed him. "Will you stay for a while?"

He nuzzled the top of her head. "If that's what you want."

"It is."

Within no time Gina dozed off, content to be in her rival's protective arms.

Flint awakened later that evening, realizing he'd fallen asleep on Gina's bed. He flipped on a night-light and blinked to clear his vision.

Gina lay beside him, her eyes closed and her hair tangled around her face. She looked so vulnerable, so pale, so different from the woman who'd teased him at the dance club.

Tempted to hold her again, he reached out, then drew back, suddenly confused. As usual, she played havoc with his emotions.

He needed to get out of here, to go home and get his head straight.

Rising, he took care not to stir the mattress. But when his booted feet sounded against the hardwood floor, Gina woke up.

"Flint?" She gazed at him through shadowed eyes. "Don't leave. Not yet."

He stopped, struck by the quaver in her voice. "I wasn't," he lied. "I was just getting out of bed."

She sat up and pushed her hair away from her face, but several curls refused to comply. "Did you fall asleep, too?"

"Yeah." And he felt awkward about it. Somehow, sleeping in the same bed seemed more intimate than all the kissing and touching they'd done. And he wasn't comfortable feeling that close to her.

True, she was far more vulnerable than he'd ever imagined. She had an angelic side to go along with the devil in her, but she was still a career-minded woman.

Like his mother. And Tara, of course.

But at the time he'd been seeing Tara, he hadn't known the truth about his mom. Things were different now. What his mom had done had changed him.

"You were going home, weren't you?" Gina hugged a pillow to her chest. "Without saying goodbye?"

"No, I wasn't." Another lie. Another mark on his soul.

"Yes, you were. And just when I thought we were actually becoming friends."

Damn it, he thought. She looked mortally wounded, and that made him feel like a heel. He wanted to protect her, yet he wanted to push her away, to keep her at arm's length. Nothing was simple where Gina was concerned. Nothing at all.

"Friends?" He crossed his arms and heaved a rough breath. "Does that mean you don't hate me anymore?"

"Do you still hate me?"

He gave her a suspicious look. "You first."

She gnawed on her lip. "I never really did, I guess. I was just mad at you."

"Dogs get mad. People get angry," he responded, skirting around the subject.

"Don't correct my grammar. And answer the stupid question."

"Okay. I don't hate you, either." He liked her. Too damn much. But as to why, he wasn't quite sure.

"Will you fix me dinner?" she asked. "And serve it to me in bed?"

He almost laughed. She was a clever one, all right. "I suppose I could do that. But you have to return the favor sometime."

She smiled at him, and like an idiot, he wished he could kiss her.

"Thanks," she said.

"Don't thank me yet. You haven't tasted my cooking."

"I was thanking you for letting me confide in you. And for promising to keep quiet about it."

"Your family would understand, Gina."

"No, they wouldn't."

"I thought you were close to your sisters."

"I am. But they might slip up and tell my mom, and then she'd tell my dad. And if he knew I had an ulcer, he'd think I couldn't handle my job." She sat up a little straighter. "And I can. I'm darn good at what I do."

He didn't doubt that for a minute. "What are you in the mood to eat?"

"Something easy on the stomach."

"Which is?"

"How about chicken soup?"

He inclined his head. "I hope you mean the canned kind." Because he didn't have the slightest idea how to prepare soup from scratch.

"Of course not. I was talking about the real stuff."

"Sorry. That's not possible. How about just plain old

boiled chicken instead? And maybe a few bland vegetables?''

''Okay.'' She snuggled under the covers, wiggling her toes. ''I'm sure I'll be feeling better soon. And then we can face the vultures together.''

''Just take care of yourself.'' He turned away, knowing the media frenzy wouldn't be easy to bear, not for either of them.

The following afternoon, Flint needed to get away, so he drove to the country to see his grandmother.

He sat next to her on a floral-printed sofa, watching her repair a section of damaged beads on his regalia vest, an intricate garment she'd made for him several years before. Her hands, marred with liver spots, spoke of her age, even though she worked with deft precision.

Nĭsh'kĭ was a handsome lady, graced with exotic features and salt-and-pepper hair, which she routinely wore in a single braid down the center of her back.

Her home represented the beauty and simplicity of her lifestyle. She didn't fill the old farmhouse with Indian artifacts like some Native people did, but Flint saw traces of her ancestry scattered about. She took pride in being *Tsistsistas*—a term the traditional Cheyenne often used to refer to themselves rather than the tribal name history had given them.

''I saw those pictures,'' she said, slanting him a hawkish look.

Flint blew a windy breath. He knew *Nĭsh'kĭ* would disapprove of the tabloid photos, but she was a conservative woman who didn't understand the spin doctor in him.

''They weren't real,'' he explained. ''It was a publicity stunt.''

''They certainly looked real to me.''

''Well, they weren't. The whole thing was a scam. Gina's family hired me to divert the press.''

Nĭsh'kĭ adjusted the vest on her lap. "They hired you to pose half-naked with their daughter?"

"No. That was my idea." He gazed at his grandmother and saw her lips twitch. Suddenly he realized she was teasing him, making him pay for his public display.

Crafty old woman, he thought.

"That's what I figured," she said. "You like this girl."

He nearly squirmed, feeling like a kid who'd gotten caught with his hand in the cookie jar. "I'm attracted to her. But it's no big deal."

She threaded another bead onto the needle. "It must be a big deal. Or why else would you do that to yourself? Especially after the last one."

The last one. He knew *Nĭsh'kĭ* referred to Tara. His grandmother hadn't been pleased that he'd taken up with a Hollywood actress all those years ago. But she hadn't been pleased when her daughter had left the reservation to pursue an acting career, either.

Of course, they never talked about Flint's mother. Danielle was gone, and that was that. The Cheyenne, the *Tsistsistas,* didn't speak of the dead. What Flint knew about his mom, he'd learned from his father.

"So tell me about Gina," she said.

"I don't know what to say. She confuses me."

"You didn't look confused in those pictures."

"*Nĭsh'kĭ,* knock it off. I'm a grown man. I don't need this."

She chuckled under her breath. "So, when do I get to meet her? This Gina who confuses you?"

"You won't. Our scandal will be over soon."

"How soon?"

"I'm not sure." It depended on Gina's health, but he wasn't at liberty to say. He'd promised to keep her secret.

"Then why can't I meet her next week?"

Was his grandmother playing matchmaker? Or was she

simply curious about the woman he'd been photographed with? "I don't know what I'll be doing next week."

"You'll be at the church powwow with me."

Damn. He'd forgotten all about the one-day event *Nĭsh'kĭ* church sponsored. "I'm not sure I can go."

"Then why did you bring me your vest?" She shoved the beadwork under his nose.

"Because it was damaged, and you always repair my regalia."

She put her hand on his knee. "When's the last time you danced, Flint?"

"It's been months. But you know how busy I am." He sat for a moment, missing the powwow circle in which he'd been raised. His grandmother had moved to Massachusetts after his mother had died, and she'd taught him to honor the Drum. "Okay, I'll be there. But I'm not bringing Gina."

He wasn't prepared to invite her into his scared circle. Because that would be like inviting Gina Barone straight into his heart.

Seven

Gina's life spun out of control in the next two days. Private citizens asked for her autograph, and reporters dogged her every move. They waited outside the brownstone every morning to catch her on the way to work. They snapped candid photos, shoved microphones in her face and asked intrusive questions.

Questions about Flint. And Tara Shaw. Supposedly Tara and her current husband were having problems, which, according to the press, meant that Tara would probably seek out Flint. For comfort. And for sex.

The reporters wanted to know what Gina intended to do about it. Would she battle Tara for Flint? Would there be a catfight?

Gina turned to look at Flint. They walked hand-in-hand through an antique show, giving Boston and the rest of the world plenty to talk about.

He nuzzled her neck every time they stopped to view a

rare table or an ornate cabinet. And she, of course, returned his outward affection.

Gina played her part, even though she wanted to scream. The Tara Shaw mystery was driving her crazy, and the media fueled the fire, making her wonder what Flint was hiding.

"Let's check this out." Flint steered Gina toward a vintage jewelry display, then glanced over his shoulder.

"Is our shadow there?" she asked, knowing he was checking to see if a local cameraman still followed them.

"Yep."

She sighed. The photographer had been a constant tag, an annoying tail. "What kind of pictures does he expect to get? After all, we're in a public setting."

Flint grinned. "Maybe he thinks we're going to do it, right in front of everyone."

"Very funny." She tried to keep her tone light, but she couldn't get Tara off her mind. What if the other woman really did come looking for Flint? What if she pressed those massive breasts against his chest and cried on his shoulder? The actress might be twenty-one years his senior, but she'd aged like a fine wine. Then again, she'd probably gotten a little help. A tuck here, a nip there. Beverly Hills overflowed with cosmetic surgeons, and Tara could afford the best.

Gina moved closer to Flint, making sure no one else was within earshot. "Did I tell you I was solicited by a men's magazine?"

"Really? Did they want an interview?"

"No. They asked if I was interested in doing a celebrity layout. A nude pictorial." They'd also informed her that Tara Shaw had appeared in their July, 1975 issue, posing in a feather boa and platforms.

For a moment Flint fell silent. And then he simply said, "Wow."

Wow? What was that supposed to mean? That she wasn't

sexy enough to make the grade? "I told them I would think about it."

His mouth snaked into a grin. "You're kidding?"

Gina wanted to kick him, but instead she tossed a stray curl over her shoulder. She'd taken to wearing her hair loose, at least during their public outings. And why not? The media had dubbed her a "bohemian-haired beauty," and she'd decided not to spoil her new, dangerous image. "I could pull it off if I wanted to."

His grin widened. "I don't doubt that for a second."

Surprised by his reaction, she met his gaze. "So you think I'd make a good nude model?" *As good as Tara Shaw?* she wanted to add.

"Hell, yes."

He brushed his body against hers, making her warm. When she brushed back, he kissed her.

The lady manning the jewelry counter gasped, but Gina didn't care. She slipped her tongue into Flint's mouth and tasted his desire.

A hunger that seemed much too real to be staged.

When the kiss ended, Gina kept her arms around him, even though an elderly couple walked by and gave her a disgusted look and a biker-type guy flashed a thumbs-up. The photographer lurked at the next booth, framing the entire scene for another shot.

"Do you know what the current gossip is?" Flint asked. "Hot off today's presses?"

"No. What?"

"That we made a sex tape."

Gina's breath rushed out. "A porno?"

"A private tape of us making love," he clarified.

That sounded like the same thing to her. "How do you know that's what they're saying?"

He flashed his spin-doctor smile. "I have connections."

She studied his smile, keeping her voice to a whisper. The cameraman probably thought she was begging Flint to

take her home and have his wicked way with her. On film.
"You didn't start that story, did you?"

"Me? No way. I just heard about it, that's all."

Gina tilted her head. Where Flint was concerned, she
didn't know what to believe. "Are you telling me the
truth?"

Suddenly evasive, he let her go and turned toward the
jewelry display.

The woman behind the counter, the stunned female
who'd gasped earlier, watched him in awe.

As he scanned the colorful gems behind the glass, Gina
slipped her hands in her pockets and tried not to focus on
how this scandal would affect the rest of her life. She
wasn't a movie star, like Tara Shaw. She was just an Italian
girl from Boston lucky enough to be born into a wealthy
family. A rich girl with an ulcer and unruly hair. How
glamorous could that be?

She turned and found herself besieged by at least a hun-
dred pairs of curious eyes. About fifty people gathered near
the jewelry booth, watching and waiting for something exciting to happen.

Flint pointed to an item in the case. "May I see that?"

"Certainly." The saleswoman removed a pendant and
handed it to him. She was a mousy-looking brunette with
wire-rimmed glasses and fading makeup, but she made a
point of smiling at him. When he smiled back at her, she
all but swooned.

"I'll take it," he said a moment later. "The necklace,"
he added, when the woman merely stared.

"Oh, of course." She rang up the sale, quoting an astro-
nomical price.

He paid with a credit card and walked over to Gina. "For
you, milady."

She glanced at the gift he'd pressed into her hand—a
diamond-and-platinum cherub shining on the end of a glittering chain. Flint had bought her an angel.

* * *

Several hours later Flint weaved in and out of traffic. Gina sat next to him, fingering the pendant around her neck. It was foolish, she knew, to feel sentimental about his gift, but she couldn't help it.

What a complex man he was. Demanding, funny, aloof. Even romantic, she thought, clutching the cherub.

He checked the rearview mirror. "Guess who's behind us?"

She didn't need to guess. "The pesky photographer."

"The very one. Boy, is that guy persistent."

"Did you know it would be like this?" she asked. "Did you know the press would be so relentless?"

"Pretty much. I've been through this before."

"Of course. With Tara." The actress who'd been troubling her for most of the day. "They keep comparing me to her."

He glanced at his mirror again. "I know. Do you want me to try to lose this guy?"

Gina crossed her arms. How easily he'd dodged the Tara issue. "This is really bothering me."

"Me, too. He's been nipping at our heels for days."

"I was talking about Tara."

Flint frowned and shifted gears. "She's a movie star. She fascinates the press."

"What does that mean? That you knew they would drag her into our affair?"

"Not to this degree, but I knew her name would surface."

Gina studied his profile. He stared out the windshield, eyes fixed on the road. "Have you heard from her?" she asked.

"No."

"Do you expect to?"

"No," he said again.

Trying to get information from him was like pulling teeth

from a dinosaur. "Do you think she's upset? After all, they're saying that she and I will eventually end up fighting over you."

"I doubt the rumors bother her. Tara thrives on publicity."

"She's a married woman, Flint."

"So? Her husband is a celebrity, too. And his career is floundering right now. Sometimes in that business ignominious press is better than none at all."

Gina didn't think so, but what did she know of Hollywood? Or the type of man Tara had married?

"What about you?" she asked.

"What about me?" Flint countered.

"Do you thrive on publicity?"

He turned and shot her a frustrated look. "Of course not. I came up with this scandal because I knew it would work. And that's part of my job, Gina. Making scandals happen, diverting the press."

She sighed, and he blew a windy breath. They sat in silence for a while. Flint kept checking his mirror, and Gina knew the photographer was still on their trail.

Finally, he said, "Are you mad at me?"

"Dogs get mad," she quipped, recalling the line he'd tossed at her last week. "People get angry."

He broke into a grin. "Touché, milady. Touché."

Damn that smile of his. It drove her mad. Not angry.

"I'm really attracted to you, Gina. That part of our affair is real."

She touched the angel again. "I know. For me, too."

"Then why are we always fighting?"

"Because you're a pain in the rear," she told him.

"Oh, yeah?" He was still smiling. "Well, so are you."

Gina wanted to kiss him, to put her mouth against that cocky smile, those curved lips.

He turned onto a tree-lined street where multistoried houses loomed through an abundance of foliage. Most of

Get FREE BOOKS and a FREE GIFT when you play the...

LAS VEGAS

GAME

7

Just scratch off the gold box with a coin. Then check below to see the gifts you get!

YES! I have scratched off the gold Box. Please send me my **2 FREE BOOKS** and **gift for which I qualify.** I understand that I am under no obligation to purchase any books as explained on the back of this card.

◄ DETACH AND MAIL CARD TODAY! ►

326 SDL DUYF   225 SDL DUYV

FIRST NAME   LAST NAME

ADDRESS

APT.#   CITY

STATE/PROV.   ZIP/POSTAL CODE

(S-D-03/03)

| 7 | 7 | 7 | Worth TWO FREE BOOKS plus a BONUS Mystery Gift! |

| 🍒 | 🍒 | 🍒 | Worth TWO FREE BOOKS! |

| 🔔 | 🔔 | ♣ | TRY AGAIN! |

Visit us online at
www.eHarlequin.com

BUSINESS REPLY MAIL
FIRST-CLASS MAIL   PERMIT NO. 717-003   BUFFALO, NY

POSTAGE WILL BE PAID BY ADDRESSEE

SILHOUETTE READER SERVICE
3010 WALDEN AVE
PO BOX 1867
BUFFALO NY 14240-9952

NO POSTAGE
NECESSARY
IF MAILED
IN THE
UNITED STATES

the structures were brick, with large, manicured lawns. The neighborhood held an affluent air, but she sensed warmth, as well.

"I'm leading that cameraman right to my front door," he said. "I must be crazy."

And she must be crazy for wanting to kiss Flint.

He entered the driveway of an impressive home. The windows were stained glass, and the slates and stones that made up the two-story building embodied an alluring passage of time. The historic estate had been remodeled to reflect an artistic yet traditional style.

He parked the Corvette at a careless angle. "Maybe we should give the guy a photo op. You know, something juicy."

She checked the side mirror. A blue SUV pulled to a stop on the curbless street, but not in a blatant position. She assumed the driver tried to mask his appearance, shadowing part of the vehicle beneath an enormous tree. Apparently he didn't think he'd been found out. "We're going to accommodate that jerk?"

"Why not? He's fueling our scandal. Do you realize the newspapers have barely mentioned the pepper fiasco? No one seems to care about who spiced the gelato anymore. They care more about who's spicing the sheets." He sent her his signature grin. "And that's us, babe. You and me."

"So what do we do? Make out in the car?"

"No. On the porch. That'll give him a better view."

Gina's heart raced. "Sounds like a plan."

They ascended the porch, teasing each other with playful little nudges. Deep down, Gina knew this was more than a photo op. She wanted to touch Flint, and he wanted to touch her.

He jammed his keys into his front pocket. "I'll bet you can't take the keys away from me."

She glanced at his jeans. "I'll bet I can."

"Then go for it."

She reached down, but he caught her wrist. They wrestled like kids, bumping the porch rail and laughing. She managed to free herself and dig into his pocket. And when she latched onto the keys, he grabbed her other hand and pressed it against his fly.

Her heartbeat went haywire.

She toyed with his zipper, and he unbuttoned the top of her blouse just a little, just enough to send the brisk March air racing over her skin.

Suddenly he kissed her—in fury, in power, in a need neither of them could deny.

The wind kicked up, disheveling her hair and rippling his shirt. He moved his mouth lower, but not low enough. She wanted him to lick the tip of her breasts, to ease the ache, but her clothes hindered him.

And his clothes hindered her.

She popped the button on his jeans, then realized what she was doing. A photographer was out there, framing their foreplay.

"We have to stop."

"Just one more kiss," he said.

She clung to his belt loops. Yes, just one more kiss.

His beard stubble scraped her jaw. His breath warmed her cheek. One kiss turned into two, and she rocked against him, too dizzy to speak.

He fisted his keys and fumbled with the lock. Finally he made a clumsy connection, and the door opened.

Together, they stumbled into the entryway, still wrapped in each other's arms. He kicked the door shut.

And then a moment of clarity hit. The jig was up. No one could see them now.

He pulled back and dragged a shaky hand through his hair. She tried to focus on his house, but all she saw was a blur of antiques and a maze of color.

Blinking, she stared at a stained-glass window, but she wasn't able to discern the design. A few minutes later, she shifted her gaze to find Flint watching her with a look so intense he took her breath away.

"Tell me you want what I want, Gina. Tell me I'm not alone."

A chill streaked through her.

"Tell me," he implored, his voice edged with need.

"You're not alone, Flint. I want what you want." Desperately. So badly, she hurt.

He moved closer, then stopped when they were inches apart. "Now tell me that it won't matter afterward. That you won't hold it against me."

"It won't matter," she said, praying that she wouldn't get attached, that she wouldn't long to keep him later. "I promise not to hold it against you."

He reached for her, and she fell into his arms. For a silent moment he held her, then they looked into each other's eyes and lost control.

He pulled her blouse open, sending buttons flying. She yanked his shirt out of his pants and worked his zipper. He unhooked her bra; she shoved his jeans down his hips.

Next, they kicked off their shoes and nearly stumbled in their haste. And somehow, they kissed through it all, their mouths fusing, their tongues dancing, their lungs gasping for air.

When she was naked, he lowered his head and teased her nipples, taking one and then the other into his mouth. He suckled, filling her with warmth and pleasure.

And then he slid lower. And lower still.

Finally he dropped to his knees and looked at her. She gazed at him, struck by his beauty, by the flash of gold she saw in his eyes.

She touched his cheek, the roughness of his whiskers. Shadows washed over his face, giving an air of mystery to each dark, stunning feature.

Gina traced his mouth, the masculine line of his lips. But

when he nipped her finger, she got a sudden sense of danger.

Their affair wasn't supposed to be real. This wasn't supposed to be happening.

"It's too late," he said, as if he'd read her mind.

"I know." She slid her hands into his hair and combed through the thickness. She craved him. Urgently.

He licked between her legs, and she went hot. And wet. And gloriously feral.

Grasping her hips, he held her still. But she fought the stillness and bucked against her lover's mouth.

Her lover's mouth. Just the thought thrilled her.

His kisses were slick and sinful, wild and aggressive. He continued to taste her, and she knew he was as aroused as she was.

He wanted her to climax as badly as she welcomed the sensations he incited—the sensual chill tingling her spine, the flutter in her stomach, the wondrous pressure between her thighs.

"Flint." She whispered his name, and he deepened each intimate kiss, heightening the pressure. The excitement. The sexual power he wielded over her.

He would be her undoing, she thought. He would steal her resolve, making her crave more and more of his touch.

She said a fearful prayer, begging the heavens to keep her sane. But a second later an orgasm ripped through her, shattering the last of her control.

When it ended, she nearly melted in pool of silk.

Blinking through the daze that followed, she looked at a stained-glass window, the same one that had baffled her earlier. But this time, the design took shape, and she saw a naked woman, her hair fanned like a swirling rainbow, her body arched like a bow. Kneeling before her was a man. A beautiful, dangerous man.

Flint came to his feet. All he wanted was Gina—the woman who confused his emotions, clashed with his temper

and made him hunger like a predator that needed to feed
its soul.

"This might happen fast," he said. "I might not be able
to hold on."

She leaned into him. "Just don't stop touching me.
Please, don't stop."

"I won't." *Not ever,* he thought, realizing how insane
the notion was. When their public affair ended, he would
let her go.

He slid his hands down her waist and over her hips, then
brought her flush against him. She was so damn beautiful,
slim yet lush with curves. The angel he'd given her dangled
between her breasts, the diamonds shimmering against
golden skin. And her nipples, he noticed, pink and aroused
from his touch, beaded like pearls.

He kissed her, daring her to taste herself. Their tongues
met and then mated, and she made a sigh of surrender. She
looked dazed, bathed in the afterglow of a skyrocketing
orgasm.

Flint smiled, pleased he'd done that to her.

"Is that masculine pride I see on your face?" she asked.

"You bet it is." He backed her against a table in the
foyer. Straddling her on the hardwood floor was out of the
question, but he didn't think he could make it upstairs to
the bedroom. Or even to the living room, where an area
rug would provide a small measure of comfort.

He lifted her onto the table and pushed her legs open.
The freshly polished antique held a vase of flowers his
cleaning lady insisted on replenishing every week, and the
heady scent filled his nostrils like an aphrodisiac.

Guilt clawed its way to his chest. Women liked soft,
fluffy beds. They liked romance—candles, chocolates and
heartfelt bouquets. And he knew a vase of decorative flowers didn't count.

Gina bit her lower lip and watched him. Daylight spilled

in from the window, illuminating her in a color-enhanced glow.

He entered her, and she clamped around him, warm and wet. He groaned, then froze, cursing his stupidity. He'd never forgotten about protection before, but the condoms he kept in his bedroom weren't exactly accessible right now.

"Gina, please tell me you're using something."

Her nipples, those pearl-pink nipples, teased his chest, and he shivered, aching to move.

"I'm still on the pill," she said.

Relieved, he let out the breath he'd been holding. "Still? Does that mean you haven't done this in a while?"

She nodded, and a rush of excitement washed over him. It had been awhile for him, too.

In the next instant he thrust so hard he made her gasp. But he sensed that she didn't want him to slow down, to ease the rhythm. She wrapped her legs around him and held on for dear life. When she tipped her head back, her hair tangled around his hands, as seductive as wild-seeded vines.

He got an image of Eve luring Adam with the apple, of a woman bringing a man to his knees.

But I've already been on my knees, Flint thought. He'd given her selfless pleasure. Now it was his turn to take what she so willingly offered.

Danger. Temptation.

Hot, hard, hip-grinding sex.

She touched him while he moved, while he pumped his raging body into hers. She roamed his shoulders and then flattened her palms over his chest. Her fingers danced across the muscles that rippled his stomach.

Her eyes locked onto his, and he battled the urge to spill into her. He wanted a few more minutes, a few more seconds to claim his mate.

The table shook under the pressure of their joining. The

vase of flowers rattled. Sensation slid over sensation, blinding him to everything. Everything but need.

She bit her nails into his back, and he welcomed the sting of lust, the draw of blood. Somehow, he knew she'd never done that to another man before. She'd never been this unbridled, this free.

He pushed harder and deeper, until his body went taut and he convulsed in her arms. She buried her face against his neck and made a sexy little sound, but he was too far gone to know if she'd fallen over the edge with him.

All he felt was his seed pouring into her, as warm and fluid as the climax flowing through his veins.

Eight

As Flint withdrew his body from hers, Gina became acutely aware of missing him, of wanting to keep him there.

"Are you okay?" he asked.

Did she look as confused as she felt? She'd never understood women who clung to a man after sex, and now she struggled with that emotion. "I'm just fine."

He skimmed her cheek. "So, I didn't hurt you?"

"No." Gina rose, then put her arms around him, succumbing to her emotions. She needed to cuddle, to burrow against him. "You didn't hurt me."

He nuzzled her neck, and she caressed his sweat-slicked back. He was strong and muscular, and the power he emitted made her heart beat much too fast.

Don't fall for him, she warned. *Don't get attached.*

Gina took a deep breath and glanced at the stained-glass window. While she held Flint, she searched for the naked woman and her lover, but the images didn't appear.

How could that be?

"I could have sworn…"

Flint lifted his head. "What?"

"I thought I saw a picture of a woman on that window, but now she's gone." And so was the man, she realized.

"Really?" He turned, and together they studied the translucent panels. "It was just an illusion," he said. "Stained glass has a way of creating magic."

"It seemed so real." She tried to bring the woman back to life, but all she saw were abstract shapes.

The lady and her lover had disappeared, reminding Gina that her affair with Flint would soon seem like an illusion, as well. Magic that wasn't meant to be.

She picked up her panties off the floor and slipped them on, then went after her bra.

He followed suit and reached for his boxers, but that was as far as they got. Before she could don her blouse, he took her hand.

"Are you hungry?" he asked. "We can fix a snack and climb into bed for a while."

She couldn't refuse, not his charming smile or his cozy suggestion. "That sounds perfect."

Dressed in their underwear, they rummaged through his kitchen and prepared a tray of whatever they could find. Flint produced a loaf of French bread, and Gina sliced a block of Cheddar cheese into thick, sandwich-size squares. He poured her an ice-cold soda and grabbed a beer for himself. She opened a can of fruit cocktail and spooned the contents into two bowls.

After they ascended the spiral staircase and entered the master bedroom, goose bumps raced up her arms. His room was nearly identical to hers. And even though she'd been forewarned, the impact of seeing it overwhelmed her.

But just momentarily. He set the tray on a nightstand and coaxed her into bed, where she slipped into the gentle, post-sex comfort he provided.

He handed her a slice of bread and a hunk of cheese,

and she spilled crumbs onto the quilt, realizing they'd both forgotten napkins.

"We should probably work out the details of our final fight," he said.

"Our final fight?"

"The public breakup."

A sharp pain lanced her chest. Had he done that deliberately? Had he meant to spoil the intimacy? To remind her that none of this was real? "That's your area of expertise," she said, hoping she sounded more unaffected than she felt. "You're the spin doctor."

"I guess it could happen at the Gatsby party my stepmother hosts every year. I'll make sure some reporters are on hand." He studied his beer. "Better yet, I'll start a rumor that Tara might show up. That'll have the press clamoring for an invite."

Stunned, Gina could only stare. "Won't that ruin your stepmother's party?"

"Are you kidding? It'll make it the place to be. The event of the season."

Jealousy gripped her hard and quick. Why didn't he just invite Tara and make the rumor come true?

"We'll stage a fight at the party," he said. "Then you can break up with me. I'm sure you'll be able to come up with a few legitimate gripes. Some reasons to dump me."

"Yes," she agreed. "I'm sure I can."

For a moment he fell silent. Then he took a swig of his beer. "Do you want to rehearse what you're going to say?"

"What's to rehearse? You're a shallow jerk who refuses to settle down. That ought to be enough."

He had the gall to look wounded. "I'm not shallow. And I plan on settling down. Just not with someone like you."

She narrowed her eyes. "Someone like me?"

"A woman focused on her career."

If the bed had opened up and swallowed her whole, she wouldn't have been more surprised. "That's the most chauvinistic remark I've ever heard." And she couldn't believe it had come out of his mouth. "I intend to get married and have children someday," she told him. "But that doesn't mean I should sacrifice my career in the process."

"That's a pretty selfish attitude, don't you think?"

No. Gina thought it was progress, the way of the modern world. "Get a grip on reality, Flint. Wake up and smell the century."

He rolled his eyes, and she dropped her food onto the tray. She didn't intend to spend another minute in his company. But when she attempted to leave, he grabbed her arm.

"Where in the hell do you think you're going?"

She struggled to pull free. "Home."

"Oh, no, you're not." He yanked her onto the bed and she landed on top of him with a thud.

Face to face, chest to breast, they stared at each other. And then he flashed his spin-doctor smile.

She wanted to thrash him with her fists, to pound that damn smile right out of him. "What are you grinning at, you big ape?"

"You, you little ape."

He tapped her chin in a playful gesture, and she knew both of them were losing the battle. She wanted to be in his arms as badly as he wanted her there.

He stroked a hand down her back, calming her, soothing her with affection. "Stay with me, Gina."

She closed her eyes, afraid of what he was doing to her, of the tug-of-war, of the hope and harrow he unleashed. "We have such different ideals. We don't agree on anything. We're not right for each other."

He traced a lazy hand down her spine. "I know, but I'm not asking for forever."

"You're asking for uncommitted sex. For as much of it as you can get."

"I can't help it," he said, his voice going rough.

"You're like an addiction. A drug. An ache I can't control."

His admission slid over her, as hot as burning wax, as daring as candles melting over bare flesh.

She opened her eyes and breathed in his scent. She could feel his pulse beating against hers, a rhythm much too unsteady to ignore. "I'm going to break up with you at the party."

"I know." He rolled her onto the bed, so they lay side by side. "But what about the time in between?"

"I'll be with you. And then, when it's over, it's over. We won't let it linger."

He pressed a tender kiss to her forehead, but his voice was still rough. "I wish it could be different."

"It doesn't matter." She didn't want to dwell on impossible wishes. They both knew they weren't meant to be.

"Do you still think I'm shallow?" he asked.

"Do you still think I have a stiff nature?" she countered.

His lips twitched, and she knew he was going to smile. "I've been calling you an ice princess in my mind, but now I'm not so sure the term fits. I haven't quite figured you out."

"Me, neither. With you, I mean." She didn't understand why he wouldn't marry a career woman. He seemed like a modern man, but that wasn't the case. His outdated values confused her.

He reached for a lock of her hair. "I'm going to miss you, Gina."

She would miss him, too. Desperately. "We're not done with each other yet, Flint."

She slid her hand down the front of his body, then pressed her thumb to his navel. His breath rasped out, and his stomach muscles bunched and quivered.

"Are you going to make the ache go away?" he asked.

"Yes." She would feed his addiction, the hunger he claimed he couldn't control.

She looked into his eyes and saw them turn a glittering shade of gold. He touched her cheek, and she smiled.

Slats of sunlight streamed in from the window, sending shadows across the bed. The day was chilled yet warm, breezy yet calm.

She moved closer, and they kissed. He took her mouth, and she took his.

But that wasn't all they took. Somewhere deep inside, they stole each other's souls. Not for eternity, she thought. Just for the moment.

She toyed with the waistband on his boxers, skimming beneath the elastic with her nails. He made a rough sound, and she scratched his stomach.

"I'm so turned on," he said.

"I know. So am I." She tugged at his boxers, and he lifted his hips to help her remove them, to give her free reign.

Exploring his length, she encircled him, stroking from shaft to tip. And then she tasted the saltiness of his skin.

His entire body jolted, and she took him into her mouth, setting a warm, fluid rhythm.

She knew how her touch affected him. And she was powerless to stop. She took him deeper, and he shivered from the pain, from the pleasure, from the pressure building in his loins.

"Gina." He said her name on a prayer, on a plea.

With her hair tangling around her shoulders and her pulse beating wildly at her throat, she stripped off her panties and bra.

And then she straddled him.

He reared up to kiss her, and she feared he would devour her in one voracious bite.

He grabbed her, and they rolled over the bed. Her heartbeat tripped and stumbled while her breath came in short, edgy pants. He used his teeth, his tongue, his entire mouth to arouse her.

He left marks on her skin, sucking her neck and biting her shoulders. She could feel the circles of heat, the rings of fire.

They couldn't make love without going crazy, and she reveled in the madness, in the sheer and utter insanity.

Once again she straddled him. Only this time she impaled herself, taking him inside.

He clutched the bedposts while she rode him, while she moved up and down, stroking him, milking him.

He watched her, his eyes locked intimately with hers. He was so powerful, she thought. So dangerous.

His chest rose and fell, his stomach clenched, his hips lifted to meet her generous thrusts.

Then suddenly he released the bedposts so he could hold her, so they could climax in each other's arms.

When it happened, she let herself fall, knowing she was addicted to him, too.

Later that night, Flint drove Gina home. He couldn't bear to ask her to stay, to sleep beside him. Somehow that seemed too tender, too loving. Too committed.

But now that they were parked in front of the brownstone, he didn't want to let her go. And that scared the hell out of him.

He turned to look at her. "We should go out tomorrow night," he said, trying to focus on the scandal. "There's a charity auction at the country club that's bound to get some press."

"I already have other plans. I'm having dinner with some friends. At their house."

He frowned, suddenly hurt and envious that he'd been left out. She was supposed to be spending her free time with him. "Who are they?"

"Robert and Lena Marino."

He cocked his head. "The pepper people?"

Gina made a face. ''They're not pepper people. They're my friends.''

''If you say so.'' Flint knew that Robert Marino was the man who'd suffered an allergic reaction to the habanero-spiced gelato. The man who could have died.

''What's that's supposed to mean?'' Gina asked. ''That you don't believe they're my friends?''

''I don't know. I guess. I mean, you're trying to smooth things over, right? Keep them from filing a lawsuit.''

She crossed her arms. ''This has nothing to do with the gelato tasting. Or with Robert having that reaction. I've always socialized with the Marinos. I care about them. They're special to me.''

He tapped on the steering wheel. ''So what do they think about me?''

''They know our affair was fabricated for the press.''

He gave her an incredulous look. ''You told them? You trust them that much?''

''Yes, I do. They're good people. And I need to get away, to spend some quality time out of the limelight.'' She brushed his hand. ''Why don't you come with me?''

''You don't think they'll mind?''

''No, not at all.''

''Okay, then I'll go,'' he said, satisfied that she'd included him in her plans.

A moment later he told himself to get a grip. He was behaving like a teenager with a crush. Hell, he was even jealous of her friends.

He took his keys out of the ignition. ''Come on. I'll walk you to your door.''

''Thanks. Do you want to come up for a nightcap?''

He stalled, unsure what to say. What if he ended up staying at her place? What then? The intimacy he'd been trying to avoid would jump right up and bite him in the butt.

''Flint?''

Tell her no, a sensible voice in his head cautioned.

"All right," he heard himself say. One drink wouldn't hurt, and he'd make it quick.

They reached the brownstone stoop, and she unlocked the front door. "Thank goodness, the reporters are gone."

"Yeah. We've had enough of them for one day." Because he longed to put his arms around her, he jammed his hands in his coat pockets.

They entered the brownstone and took the stairs. Silence engulfed the building, and Flint assumed Gina's sisters were already tucked in for the night.

Her apartment was dark, and when she flipped on a light, he stood like a statue.

Suddenly he wanted to sleep in her bed, to awaken beside her in the morning, to climax at dawn and then linger over coffee and croissants before they made love again in the shower.

He could almost feel the warm, pulsating water, the rising stream, the—

"Beer?"

He glanced up. "I'm sorry. What?"

"Would you like a beer?"

"Do you have anything stronger?"

She removed the jacket he'd given her and placed it on the back of the sofa. "I've got a full bar."

"Then I'll take a shot of—" He paused, deciding what his mood demanded. "Tequila," he finally said.

"Lime? Salt?"

"Sure." He wanted something with a kick, something to take his mind off a warm bed. And an even warmer woman.

He watched her walk to the bar. Her jeans hugged her rear, and her hair swayed while she moved.

As she prepared his drink, he studied her face, those violet eyes and that luscious mouth.

She handed him the tequila, and he downed it in one

desperate second. Then he sucked the juice out of the lime, recalling how she'd sucked—

"I think I'll have a glass of milk," Gina said.

Flint set the lime on the bar and tried to clear his mind. His dirty, male mind. "Milk? Is your stomach acting up?"

"It's burning a little."

"I'm sorry."

"It's not your fault," she said. "I just didn't eat enough today."

"I should have fed you more." But he hadn't been focused on food earlier, and the bread and cheese they'd prepared had been a snack, not a meal. "Maybe you should eat something now."

"I suppose I should. Are you hungry?"

"No. I'll just have another drink." While she went into the kitchen, he topped his glass, then stared at the amber liquid.

What was he doing? Waiting around for an overnight invitation?

Yes, he thought. That was exactly what he was doing.

Flint shrugged off the guilt. So what? So he wanted to spend the night. That wasn't a crime. After all, they were lovers. And she'd agreed to keep their relationship going, at least until the party that would end it all.

To bide his time, he picked through her VHS and DVD collection. She favored the classics, movies that made Hollywood seem glamorous. He appreciated her taste, her fascination with dames, dolls, gangsters and G-men. But as he came across an unexpected tape, a low-budget western from the late sixties, his gut clenched.

He didn't need this. Not tonight.

Desperate to numb the rising pain, he finished his drink and stared at the cover of the movie. He knew this film intimately. At one time he'd even been proud of it. But these days it made him hurt.

Gina returned to the living room carrying a half-eaten

sandwich, a glass of milk and a napkin. She set her drink on an end table.

He looked up and faked a casual air. "I didn't know you had one of my mother's movies."

"I meant to tell you. I bought it awhile ago."

"Before we met?"

"No. Right after." She picked at her sandwich. "I was curious about her."

He shifted the tape in his hand, once again keeping his tone light. "Why?"

"Because she's your mother, and I wanted to compare the family resemblance." Gina sat on the sofa, but he remained standing. "You're a lot like her, Flint. Not just how you look, but your mannerisms, your smile."

He was nothing like Danielle Wolf, he thought. Nothing like the woman who'd given him life, then taken it away. When he thought about his mother, he felt dead inside.

"Your mom had incredible sex appeal. She should have been a big star."

He flinched, but luckily Gina didn't seem to notice his distress. Then again, she was still caught up in the supposed similarity she'd uncovered between mother and son.

He glanced at the tape. "Her movies weren't that great."

"No, but she was. I'm sorry you lost her, Flint."

He did his damnedest to mask his emotions. His pain. "I was just a baby."

"It's so sad." Gina reached for her milk and sipped slowly. "It must have been hard on your dad, losing his wife soon after their child was born."

For an instant, Flint wanted to tell Gina the truth. He wanted to confide in her, to reveal the whole sickening story. But the torment in his heart kept him from saying it, from admitting what his mother had done.

"Death is never easy," he said instead. "But my dad found someone else. He remarried."

"I know. But wasn't it ten years later? That's a long time to wait."

"He's happy now."

"I'm glad."

"Yeah, me, too." But as hard as he tried, he couldn't forget his family's deception, the way they'd all covered for his mom.

Gina met his gaze, and he knew she'd finally picked up on his discomfort. He glanced away, wondering if he should pour himself another drink.

"I upset you, didn't I?"

Yes, he thought. Her compassion hurt. "I was taught not to speak too freely of the dead. It's not the Cheyenne way."

"I'm sorry," she said. "I didn't know."

"That's okay," he responded, ashamed of the lie. Although his grandmother had always followed that practice, Flint never did. He used to talk openly about his mom before he'd discovered the truth.

Flint put the tape on the rack, and Gina rose to toss her napkin away behind the bar.

"Are you all right?" she asked. "You still seem upset."

"Honestly, it's no big deal. How about you? Is your stomach better?"

She nodded and gave him a sweet smile, and he resisted the urge to sweep her up and carry her to bed, to take comfort in her body. Sleeping with her just to ease his pain didn't seem right.

"I better go," he said.

"You're welcome to stay," she told him.

"That's probably not a good idea. It's getting late, and we both have to work in the morning."

She walked him to the door. "Are you sure, Flint?"

"Yes, I'm sure." He pressed a chaste kiss to her forehead and went home with a troubled heart.

Nine

Robert and Lena Marino lived in a modest suburban home. Flint had expected as much, but he hadn't thought too deeply about what kind of people they were or why Gina claimed to care about them so much.

But now he understood. Gina had met the Marinos many years before. They owned an Italian market and deli in her neighborhood, but their hospitality went beyond the boundaries of their store. They'd adopted Gina into their lives and into their hearts.

Robert was an animated man, short and paunchy, with a heavy accent and a ready smile. He called his wife Mama and bragged about her cooking. Lena, as charming as her husband, appeared to mother anyone who came within hugging distance, so the name fit.

Flint and Robert sat at the dining room table, sampling a relish tray, while Gina and Lena bustled around the kitchen, seasoning sauces and stuffing artichokes with garlic-seasoned bread crumbs. Both women wore aprons tied around their waists, but the practical garment managed to look sexy on Gina.

As Flint studied her long, slim frame, Robert popped an olive into his mouth and slanted him a pleased look.

"You like our girl, eh?"

"Yeah, I like."

"You're the first boyfriend she has ever introduced to us. The first special one we've met."

"I see." Apparently Robert had figured out that their affair was real even if he didn't have the facts straight. But out of respect to Gina, Flint wasn't going to explain that he was just a temporary lover, not a boyfriend.

He knew his emotions were all tangled up over Gina, but he also knew when to cut his losses, when to sever a tie that would only make him bleed.

The sound of a baby crying interrupted Flint's thoughts. He glanced around and realized that the noise had erupted from a monitor.

"Nonna," Robert called into the kitchen. "Our boy is awake."

Nonna, Flint assumed, meant grandmother in Italian. Robert and Lena were a bit too old to be producing *bambini* of their own.

Lena wiped her hands on her apron and darted down the hall. In no time, she returned with a round-faced child in her arms. The kid looked ruffled from sleep, with dark hair and big, curious eyes.

She carried the tyke into the kitchen, and the boy grinned at Gina.

"That's Danny," Robert explained, beaming with pride.

"Your grandson?"

"*Sì,* our youngest. We baby-sit him when his mama and papa go out."

"How old is he?" Flint asked, unable to determine the child's age.

"*Nove mesi.* Nine months."

"He's a nice-looking boy."

"*Sì*, he's very handsome. And if you're not careful, he might steal Gina away from you, eh?"

Flint couldn't help but smile. The little rascal, all warm and snuggly in his teddy-bear pajamas and with his wild, wispy hair, did appear to be flirting with her. When she reached for him, he went willingly into her arms.

"Our Gina, she'll make a good mama someday," Robert said.

Would she? Flint wondered. Or would her position at Baronessa get in the way? Her career mattered so much to her, she'd gotten an ulcer over it.

Lena handed Danny a bottle, and the kid gave his grandma a sappy grin before he grabbed it and snuggled closer to Gina. She boosted him up and came toward Flint and Robert.

"There's your *nonno*," she said, making the boy flash that sappy grin at Robert. "And that's Flint," she added, shifting the child in his direction. "He's my friend."

Danny studied him with a serious expression, tilting his head and burrowing against Gina's breast. Then he held out his bottle.

Unsure what to do, Flint stared at it.

"He's offering you a drink," Robert explained with a grandpa chuckle.

A drink? He looked to Gina for help.

"It's apple juice," she said.

"I can see that." But did she realize it was only accessible through a rubber nipple?

Danny waved the bottle and made a fussy noise. Apparently the little tyke didn't take no for an answer.

Robert chuckled again. "He's stubborn, that one."

No kidding. Flint was being forced to accept the offering. He took the bottle, then made a face at the nipple.

Gina laughed. "You don't really have to drink, Flint. Just pretend."

Well, hell. His inexperience was showing. He didn't have any nieces or nephews or friends with bottle-sharing babies. He wanted children of his own, but he didn't know a thing about them.

"Got it," he said, hoping to recover his dignity. Cupping his hand around the nipple, he made a suckling sound and pretended to enjoy the juice.

Danny clapped and squealed, and Flint's heart went soft. Gina caught his eye, and they stared at each other, lost in a tender moment.

"Go ahead and hold him," Robert coaxed. "See what a sturdy boy he is."

Flint broke eye contact. Was the older man trying to make a dad out of him? A father to Gina's future children?

"Maybe Danny doesn't want me to hold him."

"Sure he does." Robert gestured to Gina to hand over the child.

The transfer wasn't the least bit awkward. Danny bounced on Flint's lap, happy as a little clam.

"Do you like your new *zio?*" Gina asked the youngster.

Danny nodded, then leaned back and sucked on his bottle. Flint shifted the boy to a more comfortable position and gazed at Gina.

"*Zio* means uncle," she said.

"That's what I figured." He accepted the title with honor. "*Na khan* is uncle in Cheyenne, for a mother's brother," he explained. "A father's brother is *nē hyō,* the same thing a child would call their own father."

"Really? It's the same term?"

"Yeah." Someday he wanted to be called *nē hyō.*

"That's nice." She stepped forward to brush Danny's cheek, to make the little boy coo.

Flint told himself not to be swayed by Gina's fondness for children. She wouldn't give up her career to raise a family, to be a wife and mother.

But when she sent him a warm smile, he found himself

swayed nonetheless. She looked sweet and maternal, with her hair banded into a messy ponytail and her apron slightly askew.

Soon she returned to the kitchen, and within the hour, they were seated at the table, dining on homemade cuisine.

Danny wiggled in his high chair, eating the food his grandma had prepared for him.

Flint leaned over and pressed his mouth to Gina's ear. "Will you come home with me tonight?" he asked.

"Yes," she whispered back.

"Will you stay for the rest of the week?"

"Yes," she whispered again.

Craving her touch, Flint reached for her hand. The rest of the week was all they had left. On Saturday night, at a party his family hosted every year, his love affair with Gina Barone would end.

Flint drove Gina to the brownstone so she could pack her clothes and toiletries. A reporter lurking outside of the building questioned them about the sex tape they'd supposedly made, but they refused to comment.

Once they entered the brownstone, Flint started for the stairs, but Gina turned in the other direction.

"Let's take the elevator," she said.

"All right." He stood beside her while she pushed the button.

"So, did you start that rumor or not?" she asked.

He knew she referred to the sex tape the reporter had pestered them about. "I might have."

"Flint?"

"Okay, I did. Well, not me personally. But it came from my camp, so to speak."

She shot him a teasing smile. "You're such a dog."

"Hey, it's my job. I can't help it."

The gated door opened, and they stepped inside.

"There's a security camera in here," she said. "Gee, maybe we ought to make love."

He looked around but didn't see anything that resembled a camera lens. "Where is it?"

"I was just kidding."

"Now who's being a dog? You know how aroused I get in elevators."

They reached the fourth floor, but neither Flint nor Gina made a move to leave.

"How aroused?" she asked.

A shiver slid straight down his spine. "You have no idea."

"I know how wild you are, Flint."

"Do you?" he countered. Although she wore a fairly conservative dress and a camel-colored jacket, the knee-high boots were enough to spark his imagination. "Are you wearing hose, Gina?"

She shook her head, and his gaze roamed over every inch of her.

"So your legs are bare?"

"Yes."

"Are you wearing panties?"

She gnawed a little nervously on her lower lip, and the innocent gesture excited him even more.

"Yes," she said. "I'm wearing panties. Do you want to know what color they are?"

"No." He moved closer, backing her against the elevator wall. "I want you to take them off."

She watched him through anxious eyes, then she reached under her dress and removed a wisp of material.

He got a glimpse of white cotton and pink lace before the panties disappeared into her purse. How tidy she was, he thought. How provocatively proper.

Unable to wait another second, Flint kissed her. Her apartment was just a few feet away, but he no had intention of spoiling the fantasy.

As she moaned against his mouth, he unbuttoned her jacket so he could bring her closer, so he could feel her heart hammer against his.

Their gazes locked in a flash of gold, in a spark of blue violet. She unzipped his pants, and when she pushed his underwear down and stroked him, fire erupted in his veins, bursting like a sea of liquid heat.

Desperate, he bunched her dress to her hips.

And then they made love.

Hot, wicked love, with their clothes on.

Blinded by passion, he thrust into her over and over again. She felt warm and slick, so wet he nearly lost his mind.

The fantasy raged out of control. He knew this was more than just sex. This was need. And it burned all the way to his soul.

As she wrapped her legs around him, he battled with the fear of losing her, with the knowledge that he didn't have a choice but to let her go.

Reaching behind her, he released her ponytail. And when her hair spilled over her shoulders in a riot of curls, he tugged her head back and kissed her. So hard, he nearly swallowed her whole.

From there, they moved, viciously, violently, craving a release. They bumped into the elevator buttons, and the gated door opened and then closed, reminding them of where they were.

Gina's eyes, those stunning violet eyes, sought his just once, before she tore the front of his shirt and cried out in orgasmic bliss.

He fought to stay focused, to watch her, to make her

climax again, but he was too close. Too aroused. Too damn hungry for fulfillment.

With a rough, jagged curse, Flint damned his addiction and tumbled into the sweet, satisfying abyss of the woman he couldn't keep.

At Flint's house, Gina unpacked her toiletries. The master bathroom had double sinks with plenty of room for two people, but she couldn't resist placing her cleansing creams and cosmetics next to Flint's shaving gear. Seeing their personal items side by side almost made them seem married.

Married?

She gazed at her reflection. Was she crazy? Having fantasies about being married to Flint? He'd invited her to stay with him, but that hardly spelled commitment.

He came into the bathroom and she felt flustered, afraid he'd figure out what she'd been thinking.

"Are you almost done?" he asked.

She didn't turn. She could see him in the mirror, standing behind her. "Yes."

"So, you unpacked your clothes already?"

"Yes," she said again. He'd given her ample closet space. He'd even cleared a dresser drawer for her.

"Hey, look, we have the same toothbrush." He picked up the electric plaque remover she used.

"A lot of people have those," she said, telling herself he'd offered to share his quarters with her because the sex was so great, not because he craved emotional intimacy.

"Yeah, I guess they do." He slipped his arms around her. "I built a fire downstairs. Why don't you come down and have a cup of hot chocolate with me?"

She met his gaze in the mirror. She could hear the wind

howling outside. The calm day had turned into a dramatic night.

"Gina?"

She leaned against him. He felt so strong, so perfect. "I'll be down in a minute, okay?"

"Okay."

He gave her a quick peck on the cheek and left her alone with her thoughts.

She splashed water on her face, hoping to wake herself. She wasn't sleepy, but she drifted somewhere between a dream and reality.

Heaven help her, she thought, as she dried her face. Coming here, staying with him was a mistake. Yet she wanted to be with him, to sleep in the same bed, to share the same bathroom, to pretend they were truly a couple. Which was a foolish, impossible notion. Her relationship with Flint was scheduled to end in less than a week.

Then don't fall in love with him, she told herself. *Don't let it happen.*

With silent trepidation, she went downstairs, then managed a smile when she saw Flint's dog.

The white and tan pooch ran to greet her, twirling and hopping in an excited circle.

"Now, where has your master been keeping you?" she asked, kneeling beside him.

"For the most part, he lives outside," Flint said, rounding the corner. "But that's his choice. Russ likes to patrol the yard. He thinks he's a Doberman or a rottweiler or something."

Gina laughed. Anyone could see that Russ was a Jack Russell terrier that probably didn't weigh more than fifteen pounds.

"He thrives on action and adventure. Don't you, boy?"

Flint picked up his pet, and Russ barked and grinned at Gina.

Within no time, the wannabe guard dog departed through a doggie door in the kitchen, eager to return to his post.

Gina watched him go, then helped Flint prepare the hot chocolate.

They settled in the living room, where a fire blazed warm and bright. Gina curled up on one corner of the sofa, and Flint sat next to her.

"Doesn't Russ get cold outside?" she asked.

"He has a custom-built doghouse, and he seems satisfied with it. But if he gets cold, he comes in."

She sipped her drink and stared at the flames, at the sparks of red and gold. Was Flint that casual with all his companions? Were his lovers free to come and go, too?

"I was thinking of commissioning Lewis to paint that portrait," he said.

She turned away from the fire. "What portrait?"

"The one of us from the tabloid picture. I thought it would be cool to actually have a painting done."

Stunned, she blinked. "Why?"

He shrugged. "I don't know. I just did."

Instantly, her heart hurt. She didn't want to be a trophy. A conquest. An illicit memory for him to hang on the wall for everyone to see. "Do you have a painting of Tara around here somewhere? Is she part of your art collection, too?"

He set his drink on the table, nearly spilling it in his haste. "What the hell is that supposed to mean? That I commission portraits of all my lovers?"

She gave him a tight stare. "Don't you?"

He stared right back. "No."

"So, are you finally admitting that you and Tara were lovers?"

"Yeah, that's right, I am. But I don't see why it matters. I mean, who cares?"

Gina drew her knees up. She cared. She shouldn't, but damn it, she did. "Were you in love with her?"

When he didn't answer, they sat in silence, their gazes locked. The flickering firelight shadowed the sharp angle of his cheekbones, and she resisted the urge to touch him, to feel the warmth of his skin.

"Flint?" she pressed, as a woodsy aroma scented the air, making the romantic atmosphere seem like a lie.

Finally he said, "Yes, I loved her. But I try not to think about it. Especially now."

"Why? Did she hurt you?"

"Yes, but I haven't spoken to her in years. I was tempted to call her right after I met you, but I decided not to."

"Will you tell me about her?" She needed to understand who Flint Kingman was and what Tara Shaw really meant to him.

"I—" He paused to clear his throat, then started over. "After I graduated from college, Tara contacted my father's company, looking for a PR consultant to boost her image, to prove that a woman could still be a sex symbol in her forties. Dad was going to send another consultant, but I insisted on taking the job."

"Why?" Gina asked. "Because you were attracted to her?"

"No, that wasn't it. I thought she was pretty, of course, but I never envisioned sleeping with her. I took the job because Hollywood fascinated me, and I wanted to be part of that world."

Gina studied him for a moment. And then suddenly she understood. "Hollywood represented your mother. It was Danielle you were searching for."

Flint nodded, then blew a rough breath. "I wanted to

feel close to her, to experience what drew her to Hollywood."

"And did you?"

"Yeah, I guess I did. But I ended up falling for Tara, and that was the last thing I expected to happen."

Gina's heart clenched, but she told herself to ignore the pain. "Did Tara love you?"

"She said she did. But after we were together for a while, she told me it wouldn't work. The age difference bothered her." He reached for his cup, took a drink and set it down. "And now that I'm older, I realize she was right. We wouldn't have made it. It wouldn't have lasted."

"I'm glad you told me," she said. "That you were honest."

"That's not all of it, Gina. There's more."

She looked up. What else could there be? What was left? "I'm listening."

"Tara wasn't just my lover. She was my friend, the first woman I'd ever confided in. I used to talk to her about my mom and why Hollywood meant so much to me."

"And what did she say? How did she respond?"

His voice shook a little. "She told me that the movie industry could be superficial and cold and that I should be proud of the fact that my mom left it behind to get married and have a child."

"And are you?"

"I used to be. But I'm not anymore."

Gina looked into his eyes, and she knew he was going to reveal something that made him ache inside. "What is it, Flint?"

"My mother's death wasn't an accident. She committed suicide."

Oh, God. Dear God. Danielle Wolf, a beautiful young

woman with everything to live for, had taken her own life? "How can you be sure?"

"About a month ago I overheard my father and my step-mother talking about Danielle. It was the anniversary of her death, and I guess it triggered some emotion in my dad." He glanced at his hands, his expression tense. "I hadn't meant to eavesdrop, but I couldn't turn away. And that's when I learned the truth."

"But she died in a car accident. How can that be suicide?"

"She ran her car off the road on purpose."

Gina tried to search Flint's gaze, but he wouldn't look up. "How can your father be sure?"

"Danielle left one of those pathetic suicide notes, asking him to forgive her."

She blinked back her tears, knowing she couldn't let him see her cry. "Oh, Flint. I'm so sorry. Did you talk to your dad about this?"

He glanced up. "Yes. And he's making excuses about why he lied to me all these years. He said he was only trying to protect me, but that isn't fair. I had the right to know."

"I can understand why your father didn't tell you."

"Really? Well, do you know what Danielle's note said?" he countered. "That she killed herself because of me. She couldn't handle being a mother. She couldn't cope with the pressure of taking care of her own child. But when I was little, my dad told me that she adored me, that she loved me more than anything. He let me grow up believing a fairy tale."

Gina's eyes filled with tears, and this time she didn't blink them away. She knew Flint wanted to cry, too, but he kept himself rigid instead, his arms crossed protectively over his chest, his features guarded.

"My dad said that Danielle got really depressed after I was born. She even admitted that she was a better actress than a mother. Apparently she regretted leaving Hollywood to get married and have a child."

Everything inside Gina went still, including her heart. Suddenly she knew why Flint refused to marry a woman focused on her career.

Someone like me, she thought. Someone who claimed she could conquer a demanding job and still raise a family.

"I'm sorry," he said. "I shouldn't have burdened you with this. There's nothing you can do."

"Oh, Flint." Caught up in his pain, she reached for him. And when she stroked his hair, he put his head on her shoulder.

Later, much later, as the fire burned low and the wind raged against the windows, she tried to think of a way to truly comfort him, to help him feel whole, but she couldn't. So she simply held him, realizing she was deathly afraid of admitting that she loved a man who might reject her.

Ten

Flint and Gina had been coming home from work early every day this week, but Flint hoped Gina would be running late this afternoon. He didn't know how to tell her that he wasn't comfortable bringing her to the powwow, so slipping off and leaving a note seemed easier.

He opened the cedar chest at the foot of his bed and removed his regalia, then placed some of the components in a garment bag and divided the rest between a hard suitcase and a leather satchel. A few minutes later he unwrapped his bustle, set it on the bed and assembled it.

The large, U-shaped bustle, which emulated the tail of an eagle, was designed to break down for easy transportation and storage.

As he fitted the pieces together, he checked each feather. He'd acquired the golden eagle feathers from *Niišh'kï*, and he considered them a priceless family heirloom, the most prized belongings he owned.

Ready to get underway, Flint slipped on a pair of jeans

over his bike shorts, then turned to find Gina standing in the doorway. He hadn't heard her come in, nor had he sensed her presence.

"Hi," she said.

She wore a sleek black business suit and a feminine blouse. Her hair, twisted into a ladylike chignon, shone soft and pretty.

"Hi," he repeated her greeting, wondering how he was now going to pull off the great escape.

She looked at the bed. "Oh, my. What is that? It's beautiful."

"It's a bustle, part of my regalia."

"Your regalia?"

"I'm a powwow dancer. I've been dancing since I was a kid. But I don't compete, not anymore."

Her eyes searched his. "I've never been to a powwow. What are they like?"

That, he thought, was a loaded question. If he invited her to go with him tonight, he wouldn't have to answer it. She would be able to view the festivities firsthand.

"A powwow is an Indian gathering," he said.

"I know. But what goes on?"

"A lot of stuff."

"Stuff?" she repeated, clearly disappointed by his lame explanation.

"Yeah, you know. Dancing. Food. Crafts. Some of the bigger powwows are affiliated with rodeos, and the celebration will last for a week."

"That sounds fun."

"The one I'm going to tonight is just a one-day event. There won't be much fanfare," he added, playing it down. "It's sponsored by a small Native American church."

"Is the public welcome?" she asked. "Or is it a private gathering?"

"It's open to the public, but this event doesn't get a lot of guests. Mostly it's the churchgoers who attend."

"I didn't know you belonged to a church group."

He pulled a T-shirt over his head and then laced up a pair of tennis shoes. "I don't. My grandmother asked me to join her there."

Gina sat on the edge of the bed. Although she eyed his bustle with quiet longing, she didn't disrespect him by touching it.

"Do you want to come with me?" he asked, suddenly unable to exclude her.

"Really? Oh, I'd love to."

"Okay, then. Change into something casual, and we'll get going."

He could handle this, he told himself. Although he'd never brought any of his lovers to an Indian gathering, he'd danced in front of plenty of spectators. He wasn't making a commitment to Gina. He wasn't asking her to join his scared circle, to become a permanent part of his life.

"I'll load the Tahoe," he said.

She removed her jacket. "You have an SUV?"

He nodded, realizing she hadn't seen the Tahoe. The garages on his property were separated, so he didn't park his vehicles together. "I don't take the Corvette to powwows."

"Why not?"

"Because like most of the other dancers, I get ready in my car, and the Vette is a bit cramped."

"It didn't even occur to me how or where a dancer would change."

"It isn't very glamorous," he told her.

She removed her shoes, then unzipped her skirt and let it fall to the floor. "I think it sounds perfect. Sort of romantic and gypsylike."

Their eyes met, and suddenly Flint got an overwhelming urge to hold her. He moved forward, reached out and took her in his arms.

She responded in kind, latching on to him the way he clung to her.

He ran his hands down the sides of her body. All she wore was a silk blouse, lace panties and a pair of thigh-high hose, attached to one of those sultry little garter belts. "Will you make love with me?" he asked.

She brushed her mouth against his. "Right now?"

"No. Later. After we get back."

"Of course, I will. What made you think of it now?"

A desperate feeling, he thought. A need he couldn't seem to control. "We only have a few days left, and we haven't fulfilled all of our fantasies."

She snared his lips in a moist kiss. "What fantasy do you want fulfill tonight?"

"I don't know. Something wild, something sexy."

Something that would mask the sudden panic in his soul.

Flint parked his SUV in a dirt lot, and Gina looked around. She saw several Native American couples heading toward a community hall. She noticed their children, too. Adorable little kids wearing buckskin, beads, fringe and feathers.

She could hardly contain her excitement. And then reality hit.

"Aren't people going to recognize us from the tabloids?" she asked.

"Probably, but most of the churchgoers know me. And I doubt they'll say anything. This is a spiritual gathering. It wouldn't be right for them to approach us about something so personal."

Maybe not, she thought. But the scandal would still be on their minds. Who wouldn't be curious? "They'll probably just stare."

"No, they won't. At least not the traditional Indians. It's not proper to stare or point." He removed his shoes and took off his T-shirt and jeans, which left him bare-chested in a pair of shorts.

She watched as he climbed into the back seat and began to dress, explaining what the components of his outfit were.

The transformation amazed her, and so did the beauty of his regalia. By the time he stepped out of the vehicle to complete his ritual, he wore a colorful ribbon shirt, a bone breastplate, a beaded vest and a leather apron that was used in place of a breechclout. Along with a handful of other accessories, he donned a porcupine roach in his hair, a set of fringed kneebands and a pair of fully beaded moccasins.

He went to the back of the vehicle, opened the double doors and sat on the edge of the storage area. Silent, Gina joined him. He painted his face into a striking mask, using sticks of greasepaint, a small hand mirror and the natural light the descending sun still allowed.

She wanted to tell him how beautiful he was, but she couldn't seem to find the words. He took her breath away.

"I'm going to smudge," he said. "Do you want me to smudge you, too?"

She nodded as he lit the dried herb. She knew burning sage represented a spiritual cleansing in his culture. She'd seen him smudge every morning this week, but he hadn't invited her to be part of it until now.

He fanned the smoke over himself, then combed it over her, filling her with a sense of longing. She wanted to touch him so badly, she ached.

"I owe you a thanks," he said afterward.

"What for?"

"For letting me confide in you."

She knew he referred to the heart-wrenching information he'd shared about his mom. "I'm your friend, Flint. That's what I'm here for."

He smiled, but the painted mask made him look a bit wicked. "Thanks."

"Is it true that you were taught not to speak of the dead?" she asked.

"Yes, but I never followed that practice. I used to like

to talk about my mom. But that was before I found out about what she did.''

"I'm sorry," Gina said. "I'm aware of how difficult it was for you to tell me."

"Now that you know, there's not much more to say about it." He slipped a leather satchel over his shoulder. "What's done is done. And I have to find a way to live with it."

Yes, she thought. He would tackle his grief by marrying a woman who wouldn't regret giving up her career.

Gina glanced at her left hand and pictured a wedding ring there. Could she give up her career for a man? Quit her job? Ignore her education?

No, she realized. She couldn't. She needed a husband who respected her work, who valued her for it.

Yet there was a part of her that could almost imagine sacrificing everything for Flint Kingman.

Dear God, she thought, as she turned to look at him. What had he done to her?

While Flint guided her toward the community center, Gina struggled to steady her pulse, to take a deep breath and relax.

They passed a row of food vendors, and she inhaled the mouthwatering aroma.

"Are you hungry?" he asked.

"Sort of, but I'd rather wait until we get settled in."

He studied her for a second. "Are you sure your stomach is okay? It's not burning, is it?"

"No, it's fine. I can eat later." As they reached the front door of the community center, she realized he hadn't attached his bustle. "When are you going to put that on?" she asked.

"Right before I dance." He smiled, and once again, the painted mask transformed him into a leering warrior. A man a bit too dangerous for his own good.

A moment later they entered the building, and all of

Gina's senses came alive. The music, a pounding drumbeat and a rhythm of native chants, drew her attention to the center of the expansive room, where people were already dancing, spinning and stepping in time to an ancient song.

"We're a bit late, so we missed the Grand Entry. The procession that marks the official beginning of a pow-wow," Flint explained.

"What's going on now?" she asked.

"The Drum is singing an intertribal song. That means all styles of dance are welcome."

Gina gazed at the arena again. "How many styles are there?"

"As far as competition dances go, about four men's and four women's. Kids have their own categories."

She zeroed in on the tots in the arena. Some clung to an adult's hand, and others demonstrated the remarkable steps all on their own.

"Specialty and exhibition dances are part of the program, too," he added. "There's a lot to see."

Gina met his gaze. Flint's world was fascinating, she thought. Filled with honor and pride. History and tradition.

"I need to find my grandmother."

He led her past a maze of craft booths until he located the lady he called *Nĭsh'kĭ*.

She was surrounded by a group of other elderly women, and when she saw her grandson, she rose to embrace him.

They separated, and he introduced Gina.

The older woman took her hand. "I'm so glad he brought you. I've been anxious to meet you."

"Thank you." In spite of her age, Flint's grandmother was an attractive lady, with gray-streaked hair and exotically shaped eyes. Gina suspected she had been a beauty in her day.

Nĭsh'kĭ motioned to a folding chair. "Come. Sit with me."

Feeling warm and welcome, Gina took the proffered seat,

then she and *Nĭsh'kĭ* spent several hours watching Flint dance.

He was a Northern Traditional dancer, she learned, a style inspired by an elite society of warriors centuries before.

Nĭsh'kĭ explained that this powwow wasn't designed for competition. All the dancers, including Flint, danced for pleasure.

Gina studied him, thinking how regal he looked, moving to the Drum, to the heartbeat of his heritage. The mirrors on his sash glinted, and the fringe on his regalia fluttered, catching the beat. He carried a wing fan in one hand and a staff in the other. The articles gave him balance, she'd been told. And the staff, wrapped in fur and decorated with an eagle claw, represented a coup stick from days gone by.

"He's magnificent," she said.

"Yes," the older woman agreed. "He is."

A while later Flint left the arena and returned with several cartons of food. After Gina sampled the stew, she tasted the fry bread, then caught Flint watching her.

"Do you like it?" he asked.

She nodded. The bread was a flat, doughy disc, generously sweetened.

"I put extra honey on it," he said.

She met his gaze, and when he flashed that wicked smile, she recalled that he had a honey fetish.

Instantly her cheeks warmed.

Was he revealing the fantasy he hoped to fulfill? Or had her imagination run away with her?

Unable to stop herself, she brushed his hand, desperate to touch him, to feel his skin against hers. And at that innocently sensual moment, she finally accepted her fate, knowing it was time to admit the truth.

She was in love with Flint Kingman.

Gina awakened the following morning feeling warm and sticky. She opened her eyes and peered at Flint. He lay beside her, one arm flung over the pillow, the other clutched possessively around her waist. The sheet was tangled around his legs, the quilt shoved to the foot of the bed.

Good heavens, what they'd done last night. A residue still clung to Gina's skin.

She tried to move, but Flint tightened his grip.

"Where are you going?" he asked, his voice groggy.

"It's time to get ready for work."

"Not for me." He squinted at her. "I don't have any appointments until this afternoon."

"Lucky you." She kissed his mouth and tasted last night's treat. They'd poured honey all over each other, then licked and laved and made sweet, sweet love. "I have to take a shower."

He flashed a sleepy grin. "We got a little carried away, didn't we?"

Gina smiled. Boy, did they ever. "The least we could have done was bathed and changed the sheets."

"I don't know. I kind of like this." He pulled her tight against him, and their bodies nearly stuck together.

She smoothed a strand of honey-clumped hair from his forehead. Beautiful, crazy, wild Flint. God, how she loved him.

He nuzzled her neck. "Can't you ditch work and stay home with me for a while?"

"I wish I could, but I'm swamped this morning." Her brother had called a mandatory meeting, and she was expected to be there.

"Will you try to come home early?"

"Yes. I should be back by four."

"Good." He snuggled deeper into his pillow and closed his eyes. "I'll shower and change the sheets later."

She studied his features, the chiseled cheekbones, the determined jaw, the arch of his brows. Heaven help her, but she wanted to keep him. And she had to say what was on her mind. She had to take the chance. "Flint?"

He opened his eyes. "Hmm?"

She released the air in her lungs. "Would you ever consider marrying a career woman? I mean, do you think you'd ever change your mind about that?"

Instead of answering, he turned the tables, putting the pressure on her. "Would you ever consider giving up your career for a man?"

She had already debated that question in her mind, and she had to speak the truth. "No. My position at Baronessa is part of who I am."

He sat up and cleared his throat. "Even if it gives you ulcers?"

"I can't help it if I'm a nervous person."

"Are you working there for you or for your family?" he asked.

"Both. What about you?" she challenged. "Why are you working for your father's company?"

"For him and for me. I really like what I do, but I have family loyalties, as well."

Suddenly she saw the pain in his eyes, the knowledge that his family loyalty had been jeopardized by what his mother had done.

She reached out and touched his cheek, wishing she could make him stop hurting. And when he put his hand over hers, she wished she could stop herself from hurting, too.

"I have to get ready," she said.

"I know." He kissed the palm of her hand and let her go.

Two hours later Gina entered Baronessa Gelati's corporate headquarters. Flint's touch still lingered in her mind, but she did her best to face the day without looking back, without picturing him alone in that big, honeyed bed.

After checking in with her secretary, she proceeded to Nicholas's office. Her brother sat behind his desk, his expression troubled.

"What's wrong?" she asked.

"We'll discuss it when Dad arrives."

"What about the other board members?"

"This meeting is personal, Gina. It's between you, Dad and me." He stood and rolled his shoulders. "Would you like a cup of coffee?"

"No." That would only stir her ulcer to life. "When is Dad scheduled to get here?"

"Any minute."

Carlo Barone arrived precisely three minutes later, wearing a dark suit and a tense frown. Although he wasn't tall, he was a powerfully built man who carried himself with pride.

Nicholas sat on the edge of his desk, and Carlo gestured for Gina to take a chair. Her father, with his booming voice and masculine demeanor, never failed to intimidate her.

As instructed, she sat and waited for the ball to drop. Obviously she'd done something that displeased him. She glanced at Nicholas, but he didn't offer any brotherly signs of encouragement. Apparently she was on her own.

"I heard you moved in with Flint Kingman," her dad said. "But only for the week. What kind of shoddy arrangement is that?"

Momentarily stunned, she stared. "This meeting is about Flint?"

"No, it's about you, Gina. I want to know what's going on between you and that man."

She defended herself. "Flint and I are working together. We're creating a scandal to divert the press, to keep them from trashing Baronessa's image."

"What about your image?" Carlo retorted. "Your brother and I should have never trusted that spin doctor. He's too Hollywood."

"Too Hollywood? He's a Boston businessman, Dad, and he's very well respected."

"This scandal has gotten out of hand." Nicholas cut in.

"And you're caught in the middle of it," Carlo added.

Gina's emotions were tangled. Her father and brother had called this meeting to defend her honor, to offer their support. It was the last thing she'd expected.

"I appreciate what the two of you are trying to do. But this scandal is nearly over." She stood and faced her dad. "And I can handle what's left of it."

"Are you sure?" Carlo reached out to hold her, and she found herself falling willingly into his embrace.

God, how she needed this. Her daddy's strong arms. His strength. His concern.

She stepped back to look at him, at his short dark hair and graying temples, at the lines that marked his eyes. "Do you think I'm good at my job?"

"Of course, I do. You work harder than anyone I know. But you take too much on. You let the stress wear you down."

She glanced at Nicholas. "Is that how you feel, too?"

Her brother nodded. "We brought Flint into this so you wouldn't have to tackle the press on your own. And now you're involved with him."

"Yes, I am. But that's my choice."

Her father cupped her face. "Just be careful you don't get hurt."

Too late, she thought. She was already hurting. "I'll be fine, Daddy. I promise. I will."

Later that day Gina told herself not to dwell on losing Flint. Instead she would cherish every moment they had left.

Determined to prepare a home-cooked meal for the man she loved, she stopped by Marino's market and picked up the items she required. Afterward, as she balanced the grocery bag and walked to her car, she spotted Maria and a dark-haired man on the corner not far from Baronessa Gelateria, the ice-cream parlor her sister managed.

And then she did a double take. The man was Steven Conti. Tall, handsome, blue-eyed Steven. The traitor of all traitors. In Gina's opinion, his family was responsible for the trouble at Baronessa. She was certain they had sabotaged the passionfruit promotion, spiking the gelato with those hot peppers. Steven's great-aunt was the woman who'd put the Valentine curse on the Barone family, and the withered old crone was still alive and kicking.

Gina studied Steven's body language, the way he leaned toward Maria. Was he attracted to her sister?

She shifted her gaze to Maria. The petite brunette smiled at the Conti villain.

What in heaven's name was going on? Had they just happened to run into each other on the street? Or were they up to no good?

Gina unlocked her car and placed the groceries on the passenger seat. Was Maria having an affair with Steven? A secret liaison? After all, she had been sneaking off, disappearing without proper explanation.

As Steven and Maria parted company and her sister headed in the direction of the gelateria, Gina shook her head. Just because *she* was having an affair didn't mean Maria was doing the same thing.

Then again, she knew all too well how easily a strong-willed, levelheaded woman could fall for the wrong man.

Thirty minutes later Gina returned to Flint's house and found him in the kitchen. For a moment she stood watching him, thinking how handsome he was. He wore a white shirt, gray trousers and a pair of black loafers, but he'd flung his jacket and tie over a chair.

He turned and spotted her. "Hey, you went shopping."

She shifted her bag. "I'm making Italian."

He laughed and reached into the fridge, removing a cellophane-wrapped package. "I bought steaks. Filet mignon. I was going to cook for you tonight. I even picked up flowers and candles."

"Really?" She moved forward and set her groceries on the counter. "We both had the same idea." And she wanted to hug him for thinking of her, for planning a romantic meal.

"What did you get?" He poked through her bag. "This looks good. Do you think maybe we could combine our food? Pasta and steak go together, don't they?"

"Yes." She gave in to the need to hold him. And when she put her head on his shoulder, he stroked a gentle hand down her back.

"Are you okay, Gina?"

She nodded, even though her heart hurt. "Are you?"

"Yeah, I'm fine." Flint rested his chin on the top of her head, thinking he wasn't the least bit fine. Every day that passed brought him closer to the end, closer to losing her.

"Should we start dinner?" she asked.

"Sure." He released her and stepped back.

She looked tired, a little weary, and he wondered if she'd had a rough day.

She discarded her shoes and moved through the kitchen in her stocking feet. He leaned against the counter and watched her.

His Gina. His sweet, wild, proper Gina. She still confused him, but he didn't see the point in analyzing their relationship, in beating it to death. Once she was gone, he'd get a grip on his feelings. Eventually the panic would end, and he'd stop obsessing about her. Life as he knew it would go back to normal. Or as normal as it could get for a guy trying to shake a woman from his blood.

"I bought an imported sauce," she said. "It comes out of a jar, but it's really good."

"That sounds okay to me." Realizing how idle he was,

he removed a head of lettuce from the fridge. "I'll make the salad."

They worked in silence, lovers side by side. Finally he broached the subject of the party. "I told my parents that we'd be staging a fight."

She turned to look at him. "And what did they say?"

"Not much. Someone usually gets drunk and causes a scene. I guess the roaring twenties theme brings out that kind of behavior in people."

She set a pot of water on to boil, then stared at it. "You don't plan on getting drunk, do you?"

"No." He couldn't help but wonder how much alcohol it would take to ease the fear of waking up alone on the morning after the party, of reaching for her and grasping nothing but air.

"I haven't found a dress yet," she said. "But I plan on going shopping tomorrow."

"Do you want me to go with you?"

She shook her head. "I can find something on my own."

He frowned into the salad bowl. "I wasn't trying to dictate your wardrobe, Gina. I was just offering you some company."

"I know. But I think it would easier if I went alone."

"Yeah, I suppose it would." He reached for a tomato and gazed at the knife in his hand. He could see his reflection, a distorted version of himself, shimmering in the blade.

"Where are the flowers?" she asked.

He diced the tomato and set down the knife. "On the dining room table."

"And the candles?"

"I placed them on the table, too. They're scented, I think. Raspberry or something."

She gave him a sweet smile, and he suspected she was trying to make the best of the time they had left.

"I didn't know you were such a romantic, Flint."

"I'm not," he teased. "I'm just in it for the sex."

"Really?" She laughed, but the humor didn't quite reach her eyes. "So am I."

"Then we make a fetching pair. Don't we, milady?"

"Yes, we do."

"Indeed." He took a steady breath, insisting he would do just fine without her. And she, in turn, would do just fine without him. They'd only spent two and a half weeks together, which amounted to nothing in the scheme of things.

Yet as he proceeded to finish the salad, to concentrate on the meal they'd planned, the day of the party loomed darkly in his mind.

Like an ominous cloud preparing for a cold, brittle rain.

Eleven

On Saturday afternoon Gina went home to the brownstone. She needed some time alone, a few hours of solitude before she returned to Flint's house to get ready for the party— the roaring twenties gala that would end her relationship with the man she loved.

Like a zombie, she sat on the sofa and stared straight ahead. How was she supposed to walk into the Kingman estate and pretend that her heart wasn't shattering into a million painful pieces?

She blinked and caught sight of the entertainment center—the television, the stereo, the DVD player, the nearly outdated VCR.

Shifting her gaze, she studied her film collection and thought about Flint's mother, the beautiful starlet who'd committed a selfish, dramatic act.

Damn you, Danielle. Damn you for hurting your son, for making him so wary, for tainting his views on marriage and motherhood.

Flint deserved better. He deserved a mother who'd cared about him, who'd remained by his side to watch him grow.

A knock sounded, interrupting Gina's thoughts. She took a deep, emotional breath, realizing one of her sisters must be at the door.

What if it was Maria? She wasn't sure what to say to Maria considering her suspicions about Steven Conti.

Then again, why should she say anything? Gina wasn't a saint. She'd been sleeping with Flint, knowing full well he wasn't going to make a commitment. So why condemn her sister?

She answered the summons and found Rita, not Maria, at the door. The nurse gave her a weary smile.

"Rita? What's going on? You look beat."

"I received another gift from my secret admirer. And I just needed to talk to someone about it."

"Oh, honey. Come on in," Gina said. "Could it be a birthday present?" She hadn't forgotten her sister's birthday.

Rita shook her head as she entered the apartment, and they headed for the living room, where they sat side by side on the sofa. "No. Why wouldn't there be a card?"

"Are you worried this guy could be dangerous?" Gina asked, studying the other woman's fretful expression.

"I don't know. Maybe."

"Was the gift overly personal? Or sexual?"

"No." Rita smoothed her hair. It fell to her shoulders in a rich shade of brown. "There wasn't anything disturbing about the gift. In fact, he's never given me anything that doesn't seem well-intentioned, yet I can't seem to shake this edgy feeling."

"Women's intuition?" Gina asked.

"Maybe. Or it might be just good old-fashioned fear, my imagination running amok. There are a lot of wackos out there."

Gina frowned. "Have you considered calling the police?"

Rita sighed. "I don't think it would do any good. I don't have any proof that he's a...stalker. I don't even know who he is."

"Maybe you should file a report anyway," Gina suggested, wondering if the police would take the case seriously.

"I will, if he does anything that could be interpreted as threatening. But for now I just wanted to get it off my chest."

"What are they saying at the hospital? Does anyone have any theories?"

"The other nurses are convinced he's a young, handsome intern." Rita picked up a magazine from the coffee table, then set it down, giving her idle hands something to do. "They think the gifts are romantic. And in a way, I suppose they are."

"But in another way," Gina added, "the whole thing is creepy."

"Exactly." Rita fell silent for a moment, then she gave Gina a serious study. "So, how are you coping with your corner of the world? Are you holding up okay?"

Instantly, Gina's heart clenched. She hadn't told her sister that she had fantasies about becoming the spin doctor's wife, but her eyes probably mirrored the truth. "I'm hanging in there."

"That doesn't sound very promising."

"I know, but I'm doing my best." Gina glanced at her film collection, troubled once again by Flint's mother, by the devastation she'd caused. "Rita, what do you know about suicide? About what drives a person to it?"

"Oh, my. What brought that on? Are you sure you're okay?"

"I'm sorry. I should have explained." She looked at her sister, at the concern on Rita's face. "A friend of mine is struggling with his mother's suicide. It happened when he was baby, but he just found out about it recently.''

''Did she leave a note?''

''Yes. Apparently she became overly depressed after he was born, obsessing about the career she gave up and panicking about raising a child. Can you imagine a new mother being that desperate? That self-absorbed?''

''Actually, I can,'' Rita said, her voice taking on a professional, if not clinical tone. ''Have you ever heard of postpartum depression? Or better yet, postpartum psychosis?''

Gina moved closer. ''Are you talking about the baby blues?''

''In a sense, but to a much stronger degree. New mothers affected with these mood disorders experience a range of symptoms and sometimes exhibit bizarre or dangerous behavior. The mild cases disappear on their own, but if a severe case goes untreated, it can lead to disaster.''

''Like suicide?'' Gina asked.

''Yes. Of course, there's no way to know about your friend's mother, not without her medical records.''

''I suppose you're right.'' But that didn't mean she couldn't mention it to Flint, that it wasn't worth discussing.

Gina returned to Flint's house hours later. Armed with information, she searched the estate and found him on the patio, his hair disturbed by the wind.

He sipped a cup of coffee and watched the setting sun. The air was cold and brisk, the sky a scatter of clouds.

He turned toward her. ''You're back?''

She sat across from him, praying that she could ease his pain, that together they could uncover the truth behind Danielle's suicide. ''I have something to tell you, Flint.''

He frowned at the landscape, at the perfectly groomed yard, at the towering trees and stone planters. ''I have something to tell you, too.''

He looked worried, she thought. Edgy. Like a dark, brooding warrior. "What's wrong?" she asked, realizing her news could wait.

He met her gaze. "Tara's coming to the party."

Gina felt the blood drain from her face, the air in her lungs expand. His ex-lover was attending their breakup? "Did you invite her?"

"What? No. Her publicist called and said to expect her."

"Why?"

"I don't know. But he said that she wanted to talk to me. Privately. And that it was important."

How important? Gina wondered. Was Tara going to make a play for him? Was she going tell him that she missed him? That her marriage was falling apart? That she needed comfort? Love? Sex?

Gina wrapped her arms around her middle, pride keeping her voice steady, her outward appearance intact. How could she compete with Tara Shaw? With the one true love of Flint's life? "Are you nervous about seeing her?"

"Frantic. I can't believe this is happening. Especially tonight."

Yes, she thought. Tonight. When their staged fight would set him free. "How could she just invite herself? That isn't right."

Flint blew a windy breath. "Maybe not. But there were rumors in the tabloids about her attending this party."

Rumors that he'd started, Gina realized. Maybe deep down he'd wanted Tara to show. Maybe he had fantasies about seeing her just one more time.

"Will her husband be accompanying her?" she asked, hopeful.

"No. Her publicist said she'd be there alone. Or with her bodyguard, I suppose. Around nine."

Suddenly nine o'clock seemed like the bewitching hour, the hour Gina would lose the glass slipper her prince would never retrieve. Letting Flint go was almost more than she could bear, but turning him over to his ex-lover made every cell in her body weep.

"Should we stage the fight before or after Tara arrives?" she asked, praying he would opt to cancel.

"Damn it. I don't know." He dragged a hand through his wind-ravaged hair. "Before, after. Either way, the press is going to blame Tara for our breakup. And those gossip rags are going to spread more lies. This thing will never end."

This thing? Their affair? The nights they'd spent in each other's arms?

She turned to look at the sky and saw the dim gray light of dusk, the promise of rain.

"You never told me your news," Flint said, drawing her attention to him.

Good heavens. She'd forgotten all about his mother. Now she had to tell him. She had to bring up another emotional issue.

"Danielle might have been ill, Flint."

He gave her a blank stare. "Ill? What are you talking about?"

"There's a disorder some women are affected with after childbirth. It's called postpartum depression. And there's an even stronger degree of it that's considered a psychosis."

He stood and pushed away his chair. "Please, Gina, don't make excuses for my mother."

"I'm not." She rose and walked toward him. "These disorders can be quite severe."

"I've heard of them. I've seen things in the paper about women using postpartum psychosis as a defense in court because they freaked out and killed their kids."

"I'm not here to debate the cases you've read about. But I'm telling you, these disorders are real. Rita is the one who brought this up, and she's a nurse." Gina put her hands in her pockets to ward off the cold. "And after I talked to my sister, I spent hours on the Internet researching postpartum depression and the varying degrees of it. I even called some of the support groups to ask questions.''

''My mother was depressed about losing her career.''

''Yes, she was. But maybe those weren't feelings she could control. If we talked to your father, if we obtained Danielle's medical records, maybe we could find out the truth.''

''We? I'm not going to drag you into this mess. And to be quite honest, I'm not sure it matters.''

''Yes, it does.''

''Why?'' he asked. ''She's been dead for thirty years. Why should I care?''

Because you're hurting, Gina thought. *And you need answers.* ''Danielle could have been struggling with any number of symptoms. Some women lack interest in their babies, and others have fears of harming them.''

Flint frowned. ''Do they have fears of harming themselves, too? Is that one of the symptoms?''

''Yes.''

He shook his head. ''It's just so hard to fathom.''

''I know. But according to the experts, postpartum psychosis is considered a serious medical condition and should be treated immediately.''

''Do you honestly think that's what was wrong with my mom?''

''I can't say for sure. But it's a possibility.''

''And you're willing to help me find out?'' he asked.

She nodded.

''What if we find out that she wasn't ill? That she just hated her life. And me.''

''I don't see how anyone could hate you, Flint.''

He moved closer, and when they were just inches apart, he reached for her. His touch, his affection made her ache, but she accepted his embrace, holding him in the circle of her arms.

"You used to hate me," he said.

"That isn't true. I never did."

"Are you going to miss me as much as I'm going to miss you?" he asked.

More, she thought. He would have Tara waiting in the wings, an ex-lover all too willing to console him. "Yes."

He pulled her closer, so close their bodies were nearly one.

She drew a shaky breath. How could he torture her like this? How could he pretend that Tara wasn't there, like a ghost drifting between them?

"We should get ready," she said. "We're expected at your parents' house by seven."

"It doesn't matter. We can be late."

He held her a moment longer, and suddenly the wind shifted, making way for a quiet rain.

As water drizzled from the sky, Gina closed her eyes and wished that she could find a way to stop loving Flint. Yet as she inhaled the scent of his skin and felt the wonder of his body next to hers, she knew she would love him forever. This man she couldn't keep.

The Gatsby party was in full swing when Flint and Gina arrived. The Kingman estate had been transformed into the jazz age, where speakeasies, prohibition and It ruled supreme.

It, Flint knew, was the 1920s slang for sex appeal. And everyone at his stepmother's party clamored to show everyone else that they had It.

Women frolicked in flapper dresses or glided through the mansion in long elegant gowns or pajama-style smoking suits. The men in attendance did their best to embody screen stars like Douglas Fairbanks, Sr., and Rudolph Valentino. Of course, some chose a more humorous approach, going for the Charlie Chaplin or Buster Keaton vibe. And then there were the mobsters, the tough guys who dipped their hats like Al Capone.

Flint used to enjoy this soiree, but tonight he was too damn nervous to slip into the party mode.

He turned to look at Gina. She walked beside him, as breathtaking as the rain-shrouded night. Her vintage dress shimmered, streaming to the floor like a silver-lined waterfall. Her hair, secured in a fashionable bun, was adorned with a jeweled headband that complemented the long strand of pearls draped around her neck.

Why was she so quiet, so elegantly reserved? Was she playing a role for the reporters? The regal heiress. The Boston princess preparing to face the Hollywood movie star.

He knew that Tara's impending arrival troubled Gina. It troubled him, too. He had no idea what Tara wanted. Nor could he deal with any more stress, not tonight. Not on the night he was losing the woman he—

He—

He what? Lusted after? Craved?

No, he thought. No. It went much deeper than that. Somewhere along the way Gina had become more than an addiction, more than the equivalent of a sexual drug.

She'd become part of him, part of every breath he took, every word he spoke, every smile, every frown, every emotion that made him who he was.

Dear God. Flint's knees nearly buckled.

He loved her. He truly loved her.

All this time he'd been fighting the panic, the obsession, the seesaw of emotions. The desperate twists and turns of a captured heart.

Now it was too late. Gina had agreed to end their relationship.

And why wouldn't she? He'd never offered her anything but sex, anything but an erotic tangle between the sheets.

There was no reason for her to love him back. He'd done nothing to earn that. He'd accused her of being selfish for wanting to balance a family and a career. Yet she'd come to him today, as a friend, trying to ease his pain about his family. About the mother who'd abandoned him.

"What time is it?"

Flint turned to the sound of Gina's voice. He wanted to hold her, to press her against his heart, but instead he took a steadying breath and checked his watch. "A little after eight."

"It's raining harder now," she said.

"Yes." Suddenly he could hear it pounding on the roof, rising above the music, the voices, the party that would end his affair with the woman he'd never really gotten to love.

A tuxedoed waiter stopped with a tray of champagne, and Gina shook her head, refusing a drink. Flint declined, as well.

"Gina?" he said, after the waiter moved on.

"Yes?"

"Do you want to meet my parents?"

"Certainly."

He took her arm and led her into the drawing room, where James and Faith Kingman socialized with guests.

Flint introduced her, and she smiled graciously at his family. James shook her hand, and Faith kissed the side of her cheek. The three made small talk while Flint saw his miserable life flash before his eyes.

His life as a bachelor.

Would Gina marry someone else? Of course she would, he decided a second later. She wanted a home, a husband, children. And she wanted to keep her career. Something he should have supported long before now. But he'd let his mother's suicide blind him, confusing an issue that had never been problematic in the past.

"Is your grandmother here?" Gina asked him, interrupting his thoughts.

"Yes. I sent a car for her."

"Where do you think she is?"

"I don't know." The party spanned from room to room, and Flint wasn't sure where his grandmother had chosen to be. "Let's go find her."

After excusing themselves from his parents, Flint and Gina searched for *Nĭsh'kĭ*, combing the mansion together.

Finally they found her, perched on a Chippendale settee. She watched the festivities in a tan dress and an old-fashioned mink stole.

The older woman rose to hug Gina, who all but melted in his grandmother's arms.

"Flint insisted that I come to this party. Can you imagine, an old woman like me doing the Charleston?"

Gina laughed, still clutching both of *Nĭsh'kĭ's* hands. "It is a silly dance."

"To say the least," his grandmother agreed.

They both turned toward Flint, but he just shrugged. His grandmother preferred to avoid these high-society events, but tonight he needed to be surrounded by family, so he'd asked her to come.

"I've picked up all sorts of twenties terms," *Nĭsh'kĭ* said to Gina. "Did you know that a sheikh was a handsome young man? And that his flapper girlfriend was called a sheba?"

"Those terms were inspired by Valentino. Because of the sheikh films he made," Flint said. "Of course, you might remember him, *Nĭsh'kĭ*."

"Bite your tongue, young man. I'm not that old."

Both Gina and Flint laughed, and then a disturbance caught their attention. They turned simultaneously, and Flint cursed beneath his breath.

Tara had arrived.

Twelve

Tara Shaw entered the crowded mansion in a jeweled, knee-length dress and cloche hat, her eyes rimmed in kohl liner. She'd dressed appropriately for the occasion, right down to rolled stockings and a long, slim cigarette holder.

Ever the movie star, Flint thought. The reporters flocked around her like sheep.

"I think I'll sit this one out," *Nĭsh'kĭ* said, returning to the settee.

Flint looked at Gina. "I wish this wasn't happening. Do you know what the reporters are going to speculate about Tara and me?"

"That she came here to make a play for you?"

He nodded. "I know that's not the case. But how I am going to dispel those rumors when I go off alone with her?"

"How do you know that's not the case?" she asked, rendering him nearly speechless. "How do you know Tara isn't interested in you?"

Troubled by Gina's question, he reached for her hand. They stood close together, their conversation quiet. "Do you trust me?"

She sighed. "I don't trust Tara, Flint."

Which meant that she didn't trust him, either. She thought he would fall prey to his ex-lover's charms. And that made him feel sick inside.

Should he tell Gina how he felt? Should he admit that he loved her?

No, he thought. Not here. Not now. Not while she was accusing him of being a potential cheat.

"Your opinion of me hurts," he said.

She took her hand back. "I'm sorry, but I can't help the way I feel."

Flint's body went numb. He wanted her to respect him, to believe in him, but she didn't.

"It's humiliating to have Tara here," she said. "Even if our affair is almost officially over, it still feels like a slap in the face."

He didn't dare steal a glance at Tara. He could still hear the commotion coming from the other room, where his ex-lover waited for him to acknowledge her.

"Then we're even," he said. "Because your lack of trust is like a kick in the teeth."

"So, if I tested your loyalty and walked in on you and Tara, I wouldn't see anything incriminating?"

He squared his shoulders. "No, you wouldn't."

When they both fell silent, she smoothed her gown in a self-conscious gesture, and Flint realized the reporters were watching from across the room.

Outside, the storm took center stage, raging against the elements. Thunder grumbled in the sky, and rain slashed against the windows.

"You better go," she said.

"I'm not attracted to Tara anymore," he told her, determined to defend himself.

"She's one of the most beautiful women in the world, Flint. How could you not feel something for her, given your past?"

Because I love you, he thought. "I just don't. There's nothing there. Why won't you believe me?"

"I'm trying."

He reached out to stroke her cheek, but the gesture fell short. He dropped his hand, realizing it wasn't quite steady. "Then try harder. Test my loyalty. Do whatever you have to do."

"Maybe I will."

She met his gaze, her eyes cluttered with emotion. Dark and blue-violet, he thought. As perilous as the night sky.

Finally, she blinked then stepped out of reach. Too far for Flint to attempt to touch her again.

Five minutes later Flint and Tara were alone in the study, surrounded by rich, dark woods and rare books. The weather still raged, and the party still rang with merriment. Music played faintly in the background, melding with festive voices and laughter. Flint wondered what Gina was doing, if she remained isolated or if the reporters had swarmed her, attacking like killer bees.

God, he hoped not. Gina might not be strong enough to bat away the bees, to survive their vicious stings.

He glanced up to see Tara watching him. She lit the cigarette at the end of her fancy jeweled holder, then leaned against a mahogany desk, her gaze instantly riveted to his.

"So, what's going on?" he asked.

"What do you think is going on?"

"I have no idea."

"Don't you?" Her lips curved into a small, painted smile.

"No, I don't." Irritated by her evasive game, he removed his jacket and tossed it on a leather chair. He wore a dark, vintage-style suit, and the damned thing was stifling him. "Just tell me what you're after. Tell me why you're here."

She blew a stream of smoke into the air. "Figure it out, Flint. Think it through for a minute. After all, you're a young, brilliant spin doctor. That shouldn't be too hard for you."

He winced, realizing that he'd been caught. "You know, don't you?"

"That your scandal is fake? You bet I do. And I'm also aware that you dragged me into it."

"The tabloids created all that bull about you and Gina fighting over me. None of that was my idea."

"Maybe not." She gave him a cool, even study. "But you didn't do a damn thing to dispel the rumors. If anything, you added a few of your own."

"That's my job, Tara."

"To mess with people's lives?"

No, he thought. That wasn't his job at all. "I didn't mean to cause you any discomfort."

"But you did." She sat on the edge of the desk. "Derrick and I are having some trouble holding our marriage together, and all that crap in the tabloids isn't helping. Can you imagine how he feels, being pitted against you? My former lover? A young man I once cared about?"

Yes, suddenly Flint could imagine exactly how Derrick felt, how being compared to Tara's ex-lover could make him insecure and distrustful. Weren't those the emotions Gina struggled with? The very ones she had tried to convey just minutes before?

"I'm sorry," he said, recalling how cavalier he'd been about Tara's faltering marriage. "Sometimes I get so caught up in what I'm doing, I lose track of what's really important." He paused to loosen his tie, which seemed like a noose around his neck. "I never meant to hurt anyone. It was strictly business." A sharp, calculating scheme that humbled him now. "I am truly sorry."

Tara toyed with a lock of hair that curled around her hat. She'd aged, but she was still beautiful, a woman of grace and substance. Flint had loved her once, but not in the way he loved Gina. Tara had been an icon, an introduction to the world he'd craved. Gina, with her hot temper and angelic heart, simply was his world.

"It's a hell of a scandal," Tara said. "If it hadn't turned my life inside out, I'd congratulate you for it."

"How did you know it was fake?" he asked, thinking it had turned his life inside out, as well. "I thought Gina and I put on a pretty good show."

"You did. But I know you, Flint. I know how you think. You would never get trapped in a public affair, not after what you went through when we were together. You're too clever for that."

He frowned. "I can't take it back. I can't tell the press that I manipulated a scandal for the Barones. That would hurt Gina's family. It would destroy their reputation."

"I don't expect you to take it back. But I came here to prompt you to conduct an interview with me, to convince the press that there's nothing going on between us."

"Why didn't you try to arrange this ahead of time?" he asked. "Why didn't you call me and discuss it first?"

She placed her cigarette and its sparkling holder in a crystal ashtray. "I wanted you to sweat it out. To fret about what I was up to. I assumed you knew that I'd figured out that your scandal was fake."

He frowned again. She'd played him. And she'd played him well. But he deserved it, he supposed.

"This fiasco has to end, Flint. As soon as possible."

"It will. I mean, it's supposed to. But things are a bit shaky right now."

She gave him a wary look. "What things?"

He tapped his chest. "The things going on inside me. I'm in love with her, Tara. I fell in love with Gina. And if she'd have me, I'd marry her in a minute."

"Oh, my. You mean this scandal turned real?"

"Gee, thanks. Rub it in. That's really comforting. Just what I need."

She snuffed out her cigarette. "Oh, darlin', it'll be all right. Being in love isn't so bad."

"It is if you're on a one-way street."

"How do you know you're on a one-way street? Did she rebuff your feelings?"

"Not exactly. But she hasn't come forward with any kind of confession, either."

Tara rolled her eyes. "Men are such idiots. Young, old, you're all a bunch of morons. For goodness sake, Flint. Tell her how you feel. Make the first move."

His pulse shot straight up his arm. Tara was right, of course. He needed to put his heart on the line, to ask Gina to become his wife, to bleed at her feet if that was what it took.

Anxious, he dragged a hand through his hair. Brave talk, he thought, for a moron. For an idiot male who didn't have the slightest idea if the woman he loved even wanted him.

God, he was scared. Petrified that she would refuse his proposal. "Will you cover for me, Tara? Will you handle the press?"

"You bet." She reached for his jacket and handed it to him. "I'll give the interview of a lifetime."

"Thank you." He smoothed his lapels, and Tara came forward to straighten his tie, to offer him a boost of encouragement.

And that was when the door opened.

They both turned, and Flint saw Gina. Tara dropped her hands, but it was too late. He was face to face with his ex-lover, and Gina assumed the worst.

He caught the devastation in her eyes before she raced back to a party filled with curious onlookers.

Gina pushed her way through the crowd, desperate for an escape. He'd lied. He'd insisted that he wasn't attracted to Tara anymore. But his actions spoke louder than his words.

Much louder.

Tears burned her eyes, but she refused to cry. Blinking back the pain, she kept pushing, kept shoving her way through partygoers and reporters who had been handpicked to attend this fraudulent occasion.

Someone grabbed her arm, and she tried to jerk free.

"Gina, wait!"

She heard Flint's voice and struggled even harder to get away. But his grip was too strong.

She turned to look at him and saw the pure and utter remorse on his face. What a fine actor he was. As usual, he played his role to perfection.

Nearly every guest gathered to watch, to view the trashy scene.

Gina caught sight of Tara from the corner of her eye, wondering how the actress could be so cold, so unfeeling.

Just like Flint.

He took a rough breath and released her arm. "It's not what you think. Tara was straightening my tie. I know that sounds stupid, but it's the truth."

It did sound stupid. A lame excuse. And she didn't understand why he bothered to say it.

She prayed for the strength to continue this public charade, to keep herself from collapsing. Their fight was no longer staged. It had become real. Only now she had to improvise, to deliver her lines and convince Flint that she didn't care.

"What happened doesn't matter," she said, each syllable laced with pride, with an ache she refused to reveal. "It's degrading, but I'll get over it."

"Nothing happened, Gina. I swear."

God, he was good, she thought. Even his voice—that smooth vodka-on-the-rocks voice—quavered with regret.

"I'm so sorry." He reached out to touch her, to brush her fingers with his. "I never meant to hurt you, to cause a misunderstanding."

She pulled her hand back. She couldn't bear the pain of his touch, the lies, the betrayal. "I told you it doesn't matter. And neither do you. You're not worth my time. Not anymore."

His breath hitched. "Do you really mean that? Is that honestly how you feel?"

No, she thought. No. But how could she reveal her heart just seconds after he'd crushed it? She would rather die.

He stood, riveted to the floor, gazing at her with pain in his eyes. Trumped-up pain, she reminded herself. He was only sorry that he got caught.

"I love you, Gina. That's what Tara and I were talking about when you walked in." He paused, his pain-filled eyes turning watery. "I was going to ask you to marry me. But I know now that you'd refuse."

The crowd still watched. Some guests whispered and others gasped. Gina feared she might faint. "You're not serious," she said.

"Yes, I am. I've never been more serious in my life. You've become everything to me. My heart, my soul, my friend, my lover. But you're right, it doesn't matter now. I can't make you feel the same way about me."

A flood of tears rushed her eyes. "But I do. I just couldn't bear to say it. Not after what I thought you were doing with Tara."

"Oh, baby." He drew her into his arms, and she felt his heart pounding just as erratically as hers.

"Can we go someplace quiet?" she asked. Where they weren't being watched, where the reporters weren't listening to every word they said.

Every beautiful, dizzying, emotional word.

He led her through the crowd, and as they passed Tara, the actress smiled. Gina smiled back. She had never expected the other woman to become her ally, but Tara was already addressing the press, distracting them while Gina and Flint slipped away.

He took her to a garden room, where hundreds of flowers bloomed all around them and rain fell against the glass roof and walls. Finally alone with her, he kissed her.

His body was hard and strong, his mouth gentle and warm. Gina closed her eyes and clung to him.

He stepped back to touch her cheek, to run his thumb along her jaw. She opened her eyes to look at him, to memorize every feature.

"When did you know, Flint? When did you know that you loved me?"

"I'm not sure, but I finally admitted it to myself tonight. I'd been panicking all week, dreading this party, dreading the moment I would lose you. So maybe I knew all along and I was just too afraid to face my feelings."

"I was fighting my feelings, too."

"Really? For how long?"

"Since I moved in with you."

He took both her hands in his. "Will you marry me, Gina? Will you be my wife?"

Her heart tugged. "I love you, and I want that more than anything, but I can't give up my career, Flint."

"I'm not asking you to."

"How can you just change your mind about marrying a career woman?" she asked, fear shattering the moment. "What if it becomes a problem later on?"

"It won't." He paused to explain. "In the past, it never mattered to me whether my future wife worked or not. I used to think the choice should be hers, since she would be the one bearing my children. But after I heard about my mother's suicide, I changed my mind. I forced the issue."

For a moment they both fell silent, and Gina knew Flint was thinking about his mother. She brushed his lips in a tender kiss, and he drew her into his arms and held her in a warm embrace.

"I can handle the truth about Danielle," he said. "Whatever her reasons for doing what she did, I can deal with it." He slid his hands down her back, drawing her closer. "But that's because of you. Because you're the link to my heart, the piece I was missing."

Her eyes misted. He, too, was the link to her heart.

Silent, they listened to the rain for a while, and then she thought about the party at which they'd met.

"I dreamed about you that first night. It was raining then, too." She laughed a little. "You ambushed me right from the start. But I'm glad you railroaded me into your scandal, Mr. Kingman."

"Oh, yeah?" He stepped back to grin at her. "Good thing. Because I intend to nose in on your job, Miss Barone."

"We're going to be working together again?"

"You bet. Remember that contest you wanted to launch? The new flavor for Baronessa? I'm going to help you with the campaign."

"Are you now?"

"Damn straight."

"And when did you decide all of this?" she asked.

"A few seconds ago."

He shot her another impulsive grin, and she leaped into his arms. When he spun her in a dizzying circle, she laughed again, knowing this man—this insistent, sensitive, stubborn man—was hers to keep.

Later that night Flint took Gina to his house, and as they entered the master bedroom, he smiled.

Everyone had congratulated them. Friends, family and reporters alike. Tara had remained at the party to show her support, and his grandmother had danced the Charleston, luring him and Gina into the festivities. He'd never had such ridiculous, mind-boggling, heart-soaring fun.

Now he was completely alone with the lady he intended to marry.

"Will you share this house with me?" he asked, discarding his jacket.

She looked around his room, the one that mirrored her own. "I already feel like I live here."

Flint suspected they'd been living in each other's hearts even before they'd met. "You can bring anything from the brownstone that you want to keep. We can blend our furnishings."

"I think I'll leave everything there. Except for my personal belongings, of course."

And her angel collection. He knew she wouldn't leave her angels behind.

He reached behind her to unzip her dress, and she leaned into him. Together, they removed the shimmering gown.

Beneath it, she wore a satin bra, matching panties and a pair of hose the same color as her flesh. She was too curvaceous for the flat, mannish style of the 1920s, but she'd pulled off the look with charm and grace.

He released the pins in her hair and watched the curls tumble around her face and onto her shoulders. Such pretty shoulders, he thought, pressing a kiss to one and then the other.

Her perfume rose like a veiled mist, and he lost himself in the alluring scent, in the knowledge that this woman belonged to him.

"How many babies do you want?" he asked.

"A lot," she said. "But I want to wait a few years."

"That's fine." He slipped her bra straps down, just to see them fall. "How many is a lot?"

"Ten."

Stunned, he lifted his gaze.

She smiled and removed his tie so she could unbutton his shirt. "Or maybe eleven. I haven't decided yet."

"How about two?" he suggested, hoping she was teasing him.

"Three," she challenged.

"Deal." He stole a quick kiss and let her untuck his shirt from his pants. "When do you want to get married?"

"As soon as possible."

"Me, too." He opened his zipper to make her task easier. "How about tomorrow? Or the next day?"

She laughed. "Are you serious?"

He grinned. "You better believe I am."

"Then let's do it. Let's get married just as soon as we can arrange a fitting ceremony."

Flint put his arms around her, and for a moment they just held each other.

"I love you," he said.

"I love you, too."

She stepped back to undress him, to finish what she'd started, and then she kissed a fiery trail down the center of his body, showing him how much she loved him, how much she wanted to please him.

When she dropped to her knees, Flint caught his breath. She'd done this to him before, but not in this position. Not on her knees, like a wanton, wild goddess.

Her touch aroused him beyond reason. As she stroked him, he watched, mesmerized by her beauty, by the erotic rhythm of her mouth.

He slid his hands into her hair and twined the silky strands around his fingers.

Oral sex, he thought. Sweet sin. Masculine ecstasy.

Flint's blood roared in his head and crashed in his ears. Suddenly he had the wicked urge to rock his hips, to push deeper, to encourage her to take more.

But a second later she did just that. She took him so deep, he nearly lost control.

"You have to stop," he rasped.

She didn't listen, so he pulled her up and dragged her against his body. And then he removed her underwear, warring with tiny hooks, battling elastic, struggling clumsily with a pair of hose he fought to peel down her legs. Those long, endless legs.

She laughed and nudged him onto the bed, where she landed on top of him.

"We have to slow down," he said.

"Why?"

He searched for a logical reason. "Because we always go crazy."

She nibbled the side of his neck. "But I like crazy, and so do you."

Well, hell, he thought. She was right. He wanted it hard and fast. He wanted to devour, to feast, to feed like the male animal he was.

But he wanted to love her, too. To show her that he could be tender. That he could bring her unhurried pleasure.

He rolled so that he was on top of her, so that he could take control. Holding her wrists, he gazed into her eyes. Eyes a man could drown in.

"We're going to go slow," he said. "We're going to make this last."

"And I don't have a choice?"

"No," he told her. "You don't."

She struggled a little, but he refused to release her. Instead he lowered his mouth to hers and kissed softly.

She sighed, and he caressed her, running his fingertips lightly over her body, around each pebbled nipple, down a flat, quivering stomach, across the ridges of jutting hipbones.

And then he kissed between her thighs.

She moved against his mouth, making catlike sounds. When he rose to enter her, she was more than ready.

He made love to her as slowly as they both could endure.

For the longest time they danced to a sweet, seductive rhythm, danced until their bodies peaked and they became one.

One mind, Flint thought, as he spilled into her. One heart. And one soul.

Epilogue

Gina stood in front of a full-length mirror in the bedroom she shared with Flint, her soon-to-be husband. He waited downstairs while the women in her family fussed over her.

She and Flint had chosen to get married at home, arranging the ceremony as quickly as possible. The state of Massachusetts required a three-day waiting period for a marriage license, which gave an eager bride and an anxious groom plenty of time to plan a simple yet special wedding, even though it meant sending scouts all over the continent to acquire what they needed.

"You look so beautiful." Moira Reardon Barone, Gina's emotional mother, adjusted the crown of flowers in Gina's hair, separating the ribbon streamers. Then she paused to wipe her watery eyes.

"Oh, Mama, don't cry."

"I can't help it."

Gina turned, and as they embraced, Moira's tears fell in earnest. Happy tears, Gina thought, blinking back her own.

When they separated, they stared at each other for a long, silent moment.

Colleen, Gina's oldest sister and the one who didn't live at the brownstone, came forward to take over for their mother, who was in desperate need of a handkerchief.

In all, Gina had three sisters and four brothers, and most of them were present today.

She met Colleen's gaze in the mirror. "This wouldn't have happened without you." In a sense, Colleen was indirectly responsible for bringing Flint into Gina's world, considering that Gavin, the love of Colleen's life, was also Flint's friend. And the man who'd suggested that the Barones hire the spin doctor to begin with.

"You weren't thanking me a month ago," Colleen teased.

That was true. Gina had avoided Colleen and Gavin purposely, infuriated by Gavin's suggestion. Now she would be forever grateful.

Rita and Maria smiled, and Gina suspected they were thinking about her angry fits, all the days and nights she'd cursed Flint Kingman.

The man she loved.

"Goodness." The mother of the bride wiped her eyes again. "It's almost time, girls. We better get downstairs." She looked at Gina. "I'm sure your father is waiting for you, darling. I'll tell him you'll be out in a minute."

"Thank you." The other women rushed out the door, leaving Gina alone.

She took a moment to study her appearance, to admire the Italian silk gown with its jeweled neckline and lace hem.

Ready to embrace her future, she left the room to meet her father at the top of the stairs. Carlo Barone gave her a dashing smile and took her arm. She clutched a bouquet of cascading orchids and waited for the music to begin.

"I already told that young man of yours that he better be good to you."

"And what did he say?" she asked, knowing Flint had sent her father some carefully selected gifts, explaining that Cheyenne war weapons were sometimes offered to a bride's family in exchange for her hand.

"He said that he would honor you with his life," Carlo told her, in a voice rough with emotion.

And approval.

Just as her eyes misted, the wedding march sounded. Father and daughter descended the spiral staircase and reached the living room, where hundreds of white candles flickered like a sea of stars.

There, in the center of all that mystical beauty, was the most breathtaking man she had ever seen.

Flint turned to her, and their eyes met. He wore a ribbon shirt and deerskin pants laced with accessories from his regalia. A beaded vest spanned his chest, and an otter sash reflected a shimmering display of mirrors.

They had chosen to blend their cultures to create a ceremony that represented who they were and who their children would become. At the reception a home-cooked Italian buffet would be served, and a Native American Drum would sing a round-dance song, bringing the guests together in a sacred circle.

The circle Flint and Gina would share for the rest of their lives.

* * * * *

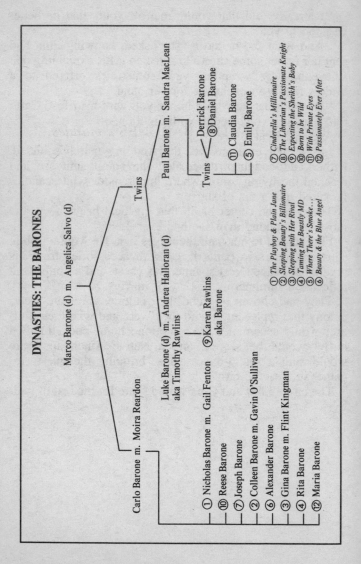

DYNASTIES: THE BARONES

Marco Barone (d) m. Angelica Salvo (d)

Carlo Barone m. Moira Reardon

Luke Barone (d) m. Andrea Halloran (d)
aka Timothy Rawlins

Twins

Paul Barone m. Sandra MacLean

⑨ Karen Rawlins
aka Barone

① Nicholas Barone m. Gail Fenton
⑩ Reese Barone
⑦ Joseph Barone
② Colleen Barone m. Gavin O'Sullivan
⑥ Alexander Barone
③ Gina Barone m. Flint Kingman
④ Rita Barone
⑫ Maria Barone

Derrick Barone
⑧ Daniel Barone

Twins

⑪ Claudia Barone
⑤ Emily Barone

① *The Playboy & Plain Jane*
② *Sleeping Beauty's Billionaire*
③ *Sleeping with Her Rival*
④ *Taming the Beastly MD*
⑤ *Where There's Smoke...*
⑥ *Beauty & the Blue Angel*
⑦ *Cinderella's Millionaire*
⑧ *The Librarian's Passionate Knight*
⑨ *Expecting the Sheikh's Baby*
⑩ *Born to be Wild*
⑪ *With Private Eyes*
⑫ *Passionately Ever After*

DYNASTIES: THE BARONES *continues...*

Turn the page for a bonus look at
what's in store for you
in the next Barones book
—only from Silhouette Desire!
#1501 TAMING THE BEASTLY MD
by Elizabeth Bevarly
April 2003

Prologue

There was no disputing the fact that surly Boston winters tended to slow things down in the emergency rooms of the city's hospitals. But that only meant it wasn't standing room only, Rita Barone thought as she gazed at the still-bustling ER this bitter early February morning. There was plenty here to keep the staff busy. Certainly enough to make her wish she hadn't picked up the shift to help out one of the other nurses. Normally, she worked in the coronary care unit, which was a walk in the park compared to the ER. Still, Rita had started in the ER at Boston General, so in a way, this was like coming home.

At home, though, she didn't have to treat overblown cold sores and ingrown toenails. No, when Rita went home— home to the big Beacon Hill townhouse where she'd grown up, and not the North End brownstone she shared with two of her sisters—her parents pampered her like a princess. In fact, she could be living the life of a princess at this very moment had she chosen, since each of the Barone siblings had collected a million-dollar trust upon turning twenty-one. But Rita, crazy as it might sound, had wanted to be a nurse instead of a princess. Now, after almost three years of employment at Boston General, she knew she had made the right choice. Because princesses, she knew, hardly ever saved lives. Plus, they didn't have nearly as good a health plan as she did.

Cold sores and ingrown toenails, here I come, she thought wryly as she leveled an espresso-colored gaze on the wretched refuse cluttering the ER waiting room. The people seemed not to have changed one bit since she had been a regular staff member here.

But then, she hadn't changed much herself, had she? she thought further. She still wore the slate-blue scrubs she pre-ferred to work, and she still bound her dark brown hair in a tidy braid. But then, why fix it if it wasn't broken, right?

"Excuse me, but I've been waiting for more than a half hour now," a young woman told Rita as she leaned way over the counter of the nurse's station. She seemed to be checking the desk to make sure there were no extra doctors hiding there. "How much longer will it be until I can see someone?"

Rita offered up a halfhearted smile. "It shouldn't be too much longer, I wouldn't think," she said, knowing she was being optimistic, but feeling hopeful all the same. "This flu that's going around has hit everyone hard. We're even short a doctor this morning because of it."

Plus, they were understandably obligated to take the most serious cases first. With a slight fever and cough, and no family doctor, this woman was in for a wait.

Now, too, they were expecting an ambulance, whose ar-rival they had been alerted to only moments ago. A home-less man had gone into cardiac arrest not far from the hos-pital. Rita had already notified the coronary care unit, and they were sending down their best—Dr. Matthew Grayson, who was something of a legend around Boston General.

Truth be told, his legendary status wasn't due entirely to his talent as a heart surgeon. No, part of his status was less legend-like than it was fairy-tale-like. Because Dr. Grayson definitely resembled a certain fairy-tale character—the Beast from *Beauty and the Beast*. It wasn't just because of his attitude, either, though certainly that had been described as beastly by more than one CCU nurse. One would think that as a result of working in the unit herself, Rita would have more than a nodding acquaintance with Dr. Grayson. But she didn't think anyone in the CCU—or at Boston General for that matter—had any kind of acquaintance with the man.

Although Rita had never been put off by Dr. Grayson the way many were, she could see why others might find him difficult. At times he was gruff to the extreme; even in his best mood, he was standoffish. His beastliness was only enhanced by the scars on the left side of his face and neck. She didn't know what had caused those scars—Dr. Grayson never mentioned them, and neither did anyone else if they knew what was good for them—but whatever it had been had done a thorough job in marking him. It was obvious that he'd had cosmetic surgery, but even plastic surgeons couldn't work miracles. Dr. Grayson, she was sure, would remain scarred for life.

But whether he truly was a beast, Rita couldn't say. Yes, he could be intimidating, but he was a dedicated professional who saved scores of lives. Rita admired and respected his skill as a surgeon, and she figured he probably had a reason for his gruffness. In any event, he'd never turned that attitude on her. Come to think of it, he pretty much steered clear of her, which was just fine with her.

Besides, it took a lot more than scars and a bad mood to intimidate Rita Barone. The second youngest of eight children from a celebrated Boston family, she'd had no choice but to learn early on to take care of herself and not let things get to her. She'd grown up with four rough-and-tumble older brothers who'd suffered every manner of injury known to humankind, not to mention their own forms of beastly behavior, especially when puberty struck them.

As if conjured by the thought, Dr. Matthew Grayson himself appeared then, rushing toward the nurse's station. In his haste, his white doctor coat flapped behind him over dark trousers, a white shirt and a discreetly patterned necktie in varying shades of blue.

"Has our cardiac arrest arrived yet?" he demanded without so much as a hello as he came to a stop behind Rita.

"Any time now," she told him.

Really, she thought, considering him, if it weren't for the scars on his face, he'd be an extremely handsome man. Standing at about six-three, he towered over Rita, something she wasn't accustomed to at five-eight herself. Add to that impressive height his solid, athletic build, his dreamy green eyes and his chestnut hair with its golden highlights, not to mention the perfectly tailored, very expensive dark suits he generally opted for, and he had the makings of a Hollywood movie star. Only the scars marred his perfection.

Then again, she thought further, in some ways those scars almost added to his allure. They kept his exquisite good looks from being *too* exquisite, and somehow made seem more human.

Of course, at the moment, he seemed more god-like, towering over her as he was. Rita fought the urge to stand up, thought that scarcely would have made a difference, thanks to the disparity in their heights. Instead, she remained seated, as if she were completely unaffected by his nearness. And she was—except for the way her heart rate seemed to have quadrupled the moment she saw him striding toward her.

But then, what else was her heart supposed to do? she wondered. They were expecting a cardiac arrest any moment, and Dr. Grayson had already surged into action in anticipation. It was normal that she be surging, too, albeit in *other* ways. Ways that had nothing to do with the good doctor's presence. Especially once she heard the siren outside announcing the arrival of the ambulance. She leapt up from her chair and circled the nurse's station with Dr. Grayson right on her heels.

In a flurry of motion and clamor, the paramedics wheeled in an elderly man who was screaming and keening and flailing his arms about. He was filthy, Rita saw as she approached hurrying her stride to match the paramedics's as she directed them to an examining room, and he was clearly terrified. As she strode alongside him, instinctively, she reached for the man's hand and held it, then winced a bit when he squeezed tightly enough to hurt her. He was obviously much stronger than he looked.

"It's okay," she told him as they came to a halt in a small room. "You're going to be all right." She didn't know if that was true, but she wasn't about to cite heart attack survival statistics for him right now. "You've got the best here to help you," she said further. "We'll take good care of you."

The man stopped trying to strike the paramedics then, and he stopped shouting. When he turned to look at Rita, he was breathing rapidly and raggedly, and his pale blue eyes were filled with fear.

"Who...who're you?" he gasped. Then he grimaced in pain.

"My name is Rita," she said soothingly, stroking her other hand over the one he had wrapped so fiercely around hers. As discreetly as she could, she took his pulse, not wanting to alarm him again. It wasn't quite as erratic as she would have thought under the circumstances, but it was still thready.

"You...the...doc?" the man asked with some difficulty, his voice raspy, his breathing becoming more labored.

"No, I'm a nurse," Rita told him as she noted the activity surrounding them. It looked as if half the staff was in the tiny room, tending to the man, even though she knew it was only a fraction of those working this morning. "But there's a doctor here," she said further. "You're in the emergency room of Boston General, and you're having a heart attack. I'm going to take your blood pressure now," she then added. When he recoiled and opened his mouth to shout again, she hastily, but very calmly, added, "It won't hurt, I promise. But you need to let us check you out, to see how you're doing."

"We've stabilized him," one of the paramedics said from the other side of the gurney, "but he's not out of the woods yet. Not by a long shot."

Rita threw the man a censuring look. The last thing this guy needed to hear was that he was still in danger.

"Am I..." He grimaced again, groaning. "Am I...gonna...die?" he demanded.

"No," Rita said firmly, gritting her teeth at the paramedic, who just shrugged off her reproach. "You're going to be fine. What's your name?" she asked the old man.

He gazed at her warily for a moment, still clearly frightened, then, evidently deciding she was okay, he told her weakly, "Joe."

"Do you have any family, Joe?" she asked as the others were working to monitor him, hooking him up to oxygen and an EKG. He fought the mask at first, but Rita soothed him, promising him it was for his own good and that it would only be temporary. "Is there anyone we can call who might make you feel more comfortable?" she asked again.

He shook his head, took another indifferent swipe at the oxygen mask, then surrendered to it. "No. No family," he told her, sounding even weaker than he had before. After a small hesitation, he added, "But...but you kinda..." He expelled a sound of pain, then grabbed her hand again with a brutal grip. "You," he tried again, "you...make me feel...more comfortable."

Rita smiled again, flexing her fingers against the force of his grasp. "Well, then, Joe, I'll just stay right here with you. How will that be?"

He nodded faintly. "That'd be good. Don't...go anywhere."

"I won't," she promised him.

"And later," he said, his voice quavering as he spoke, "after...after they's...done with me, if I...if I make it through...don't...go nowhere then, neither."

Rita patted his hand gently. "This is where I work, Joe. And you know, sometimes I feel like I never leave."

That roused a brief, if feeble, grin from him in response, but he was clearly growing weaker now. She sent up a silent prayer that he would be all right. She knew nothing about him except that he had no home and no family and that his name was Joe. But he was obviously a fighter—and a survivor—and she had no choice but to admire that. Surely, he'd survive this, too.

"This is Dr. Grayson," Rita told him, nodding her head toward the surgeon who now stood on the other side of the gurney. "He'll be looking at you here in a minute. He's very good. The absolute best."

When she looked up, she saw that Dr. Grayson was studying her with much consideration, as if he wanted to ask her something, and she opened her mouth to ask what. But Joe began thrashing and screaming then, and thinking he must be in pain, Rita glanced back down to tend to him. But it obviously wasn't pain that was causing his reaction. He was looking right at Dr. Grayson and had somehow managed to lift his hand to point at the scars on the other man's face.

"Don't let 'im...come near me," Joe said with much agitation. "He...he ain't...no man. He's a...monster."

Dr. Grayson simply ignored the comment and reached

toward Joe. Joe, however, shoved his hand away before the doctor could touch him, and began to thrash even more.

"Git 'im…away from me! Git 'im away!"

"Joe, please," Rita tried again.

But the old man wouldn't be calmed. "His face!" he cried, pointing at Dr. Grayson. "He's like one a'them…on a'them gargoyles on…St Michael's. They…come after me sometimes…in my…in my dreams. To take me…to hell. They's monsters! Git 'im away!"

"Joe, it's all right," Rita said firmly, grabbing his arms and holding them at his sides. "Dr. Grayson is here to help you. He's an excellent surgeon and a wonderful man. No one is going to hurt you," she said even more forcefully. "I won't let anyone hurt you, I promise. I'm right here, and I won't let anyone hurt you."

For whatever reason, her vows reassured him. Or maybe it was just that he was too weak and in too much pain to fight anymore. Rita gave up trying to be a nurse then and let the other RNs tend to Joe's medical needs. Instead, she picked up the man's hand once more and held it tightly, and murmured soothing words about how he was going to be just fine because he had Dr. Matthew Grayson to take care of him.

And he would be fine, Rita told herself, feeling strangely attached to the old man for some reason. Because he did have Dr. Matthew Grayson to look after him.

Who wouldn't be fine with someone like that to watch over him?

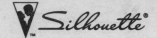

Silhouette® Desire®

Bestselling author

Meagan McKinney

brings you three brand-new stories in
her engaging miniseries centered around
the town of Mystery, Montana, in

MATCHED IN MONTANA

*Wedding bells always ring
when the town matriarch plays Cupid!*

**Coming in February 2003:
PLAIN JANE & THE HOTSHOT, SD #1493**

**Coming in March 2003:
THE COWBOY CLAIMS HIS LADY, SD #1499**

**Coming in April 2003:
BILLIONAIRE BOSS, SD #1505**

Available at your favorite retail outlet.

Silhouette®

Where love comes alive™

Silhouette® Desire®

USA TODAY bestselling author

CAIT LONDON

brings you a captivating new series
featuring to-die-for alpha heroes
from the Pacific Northwest!

HEARTBREAKERS

He'll stir his woman's senses, and when
she's dizzy with passion...he'll propose!

MR. TEMPTATION
(Silhouette Desire #1430)

Gorgeous widower Jarek Stepanov must release his guilt
about the past, open his heart and convince vulnerable
beauty Leigh Van Dolph that she belongs in his arms.

And the excitement continues in April 2003 with:

INSTINCTIVE MALE
(Silhouette Desire #1502)

Tough but vulnerable Ellie Lathrop unexpectedly finds
love with the one man who has always gotten under
her skin—Mikhail Stepanov.

Available at your favorite retail outlet.

Silhouette®
Where love comes alive™

Silhouette® Desire®

presents...

WARRIOR IN HER BED

(SD #1506)

by Cathleen Galitz

On sale April 2003

Passion is the course of study when an embittered
teacher's summer romance with a war-weary counselor
turns into the love of a lifetime. But now she must
choose between her no-strings arrangement with her
lover and the child she has always longed for.

Available at your favorite retail outlet.

COMING NEXT MONTH

#1501 TAMING THE BEASTLY MD—Elizabeth Bevarly
Dynasties: The Barones
When nurse Rita Barone needed a date for a party, she asked the very intriguing Dr. Matthew Grayson. Things heated up, and Rita wound up in Matthew's bed, where he introduced her to sensual delight. However, the next morning they vowed to forget their night of passion. But Rita couldn't forget. Could she convince the good doctor she needed his loving touch—*forever?*

#1502 INSTINCTIVE MALE—Cait London
Heartbreakers
Desperate for help, Ellie Lathrop turned to the one man who'd always gotten under her skin—enigmatic Mikhail Stepanov. Mikhail ignited Ellie's long-hidden desires, and soon she surrendered to their powerful attraction. But proud Mikhail wouldn't accept less than her whole heart, and Ellie didn't know if she could give him that.

#1503 A BACHELOR AND A BABY—Marie Ferrarella
The Mom Squad
Because of a misunderstanding, Rick Masters had lost Joanna Prescott, the love of his life. But eight years later, Rick drove past Joanna's house—just in time to save her from a fire and deliver her baby. The old chemistry was still there, and Rick fell head over heels for Joanna and her baby. But Joanna feared being hurt again; could Rick prove his love was rock solid?

#1504 TYCOON FOR AUCTION—Katherine Garbera
When Corrine Martin won sexy businessman Rand Pearson at a bachelor auction, she decided he would make the perfect corporate boyfriend. Their arrangement consisted of three dates. But Corrine found pleasure and comfort in Rand's embrace, and she found herself in unanticipated danger—of surrendering to love!

#1505 BILLIONAIRE BOSS—Meagan McKinney
Matched in Montana
He had hired her to be his assistant, but when wealthy Seth Morgan came face-to-face with beguiling beauty Kirsten Meadows, he knew he wanted to be more than just her boss. Soon he was fighting to persuade wary Kirsten to yield to him—one sizzling kiss at a time!

#1506 WARRIOR IN HER BED—Cathleen Galitz
Annie Wainwright had gone to Wyoming seeking healing, not romance. Then Johnny Lonebear stormed into her life, refusing to be ignored. Throwing caution to the wind, Annie embarked on a summer fling with Johnny that grew into something much deeper. But what would happen once Johnny learned she was carrying his child?